Romantic Times: Vegas

Heather Graham

Lance Taubold & Richard Devin

Doris Parmett

Jennifer St. Giles

Kimberly Cates

Tara Nina

Ed DeAngelis

Rebecca Paisley

13Thirty Books
Print and Digital Editions
Copyright 2016

Discover new and exciting works by 13Thirty Books at
www.13thirtybooks.com

Print and Digital Edition, License Notes

ISBN: 0692667199
ISBN-13: 978-0692667194
Amazon $10.00 6/16

DEDICATION

To all the people at Romantic Times who over the years have changed so many lives in so many positive ways.

CONTENTS

ACKNOWLEDGMENTS

Judy Spagnola
For all her hard work in making this anthology possible.

And to
Rick Taubold for his editorial assistance.

FOREWORD

Kathryn Falk, Lady of Barrow

Kisses and hugs to 13Thirty Books for compiling a Romance Anthology: *Romantic Times: Vegas*, to entertain the readers at the 33rd RT Booklovers Convention 2016 in Las Vegas.

The lineup of authors is quite varied and impressive, starting with my longtime friend, **Heather Graham**, author of over 150 romances and thrillers. She began writing Romance novels at the same time I started a tabloid publication, *Romantic Times*, now *RT Book Reviews*, and the Booklovers Convention—despite people saying I was crazy to do so.

Several name authors in this collection were also involved in the early days of the Romance genre. It was a much different industry then, smaller and less chaotic. We pushed a lot of envelopes with our stories.

Christina Skye was a Chinese scholar and spoke fluent Mandarin when she appeared on the scene and expressed a desire to write Regencies.

Carole Nelson Douglas, a prominent journalist, stayed in the St. Paul Pioneer Press office till after midnight to help the Romance cause by placing a story of the RT Love Train on the "wires," as it was called in those days. This activated nation-wide coverage for the dozens of authors aboard Amtrak, greeting romance readers (dressed in pink) at stations large and small as we headed from Los Angeles to meet up with Barbara Cartland at the 2nd RT Booklovers Convention in New York City.

Who can forget when contemporary author **Tina Wainscott** arrived at a Convention straight from Russia—having finally succeeded in adopting a baby girl (now 13 years old)—to share her happiness and tins of Russian caviar with her delighted sister authors.

Last but not least, there's no one like our romantic publishers: **Lance Taubold** was one of RT's first cover model contestants, from the Fabio days, as well as being a wonderful singer/entertainer. **Rich Devin** masterfully directed many RT Cover Model Pageants and Awards Ceremonies. It would not be the same biz without them!

RT is fortunate to have loyal friends who are still supporting us after three decades! Ken, Carol, and I are very lucky in this regard and so appreciative.

How romantic it is to come together now *under the covers*, (Sorry for the pun!) and to be writing stories about romantic times in Las Vegas.

Readers will be pleasantly surprised to recognize the names of three prominent authors of Romance who disappeared from the scene for a few years, but have returned to contribute to this collection: Rebecca Paisley, Doris Parmett, and Kimberly Cates.

The three anthologies are rounded out by a talented group of "relatively" new newcomers, including a Barnes & Noble bookseller/author—Crystal Perkins.

A huge thank you to all the authors who brought their imagination and creativity to produce the first RT Convention Anthologies.

To understand how the project developed. Every author received these directives from the publisher:

1) Write a story set in Las Vegas with action taking place inside an imaginary hotel, the Excelsior, built in 1960 by a Mafia family. (That was rather common in those days.)

2) Choose a time frame ranging from 1960 to the present, and even the future, in any genre.

Therefore, dear reader, you will encounter—at the Excelsior Hotel—a vampire, a post-apocalyptic romance, a time-travel suspense, a Fabio-to-the-Rescue comedy and more...

All our Romances have happy endings of course. And the Romance formula even in short fiction will ring true—getting an alpha male to commit!

Enjoy!

Kathryn Falk, Founder of RT Book Reviews and the RT Booklovers Convention

Kenneth Rubin, President of Romantic Times Inc. (He slept his way to the top!)

Carol Stacy, Publisher and Executive Convention Director

1

ONE EYED JACKS

Heather Graham

There really was nothing quite like watching the fountains of the Bellagio at night.

Water spouted and seemed to dance in the neon glow from thousands of lights, every droplet catching dazzling prisms of color.

Danni stood with Quinn, losing herself in the spectacle. She felt his arm around her shoulders and the heat and breadth of him so close.

"Beautiful," he said, bending slightly so that his whisper was against her ear, his breath a sweet tease. "Yes?"

"Yes," she replied. She turned her head and looked at him, seeing his smile. Quinn had a great smile. Just a little bit lopsided, entirely endearing. It had the ability to change him; Quinn was six-four, broad-shouldered, tightly muscled, and could go to battle for a cause with an authority and power that was chilling. But, his smile...

He'd suggested the Vegas trip as a cool romantic interlude for the two of them. Their day-to-day lives were hectic, to say the least. Hard on a relationship—their line of moonlighting work, their true vocations in life—making it even more so. They dealt with fear, danger, and death far too often when they were home. The *Cheshire Cat*, Danni's shop on Royal Street in the French Quarter, took up the street frontage of the historic house she'd inherited from her father. It was there that she and Quinn carried on her father's trade collecting very special *things*—objects that were imbued with evil, or, that, by their very nature, seemed to create evil in the minds of men—and kept them from doing further harm.

A getaway—they really desperately needed a getaway now and then. And Vegas!

Vegas.

She hadn't been sure. Vegas was a party town. A little something for the wicked child in every adult. Shows, music, gambling, casinos, garish lights! Not that she was against a party, or that a few turns at some wicked pleasure might be so bad. But, romantic? A Caribbean island was romantic, a trip to Paris was romantic, but Vegas... she wasn't so sure. Vegas almost seemed like a neon version of Bourbon Street at home.

No, she thought. *It hadn't really been the thought that a pristine beach on a hidden island would be so much better—it was the dream. A bizarre dream she'd had the night before Jeremy had called them... a dream about running desperately from a giant one-eyed Jack.*

But there was nothing to worry about, she was having a wonderful time—and no giant one-eyed Jacks were running anywhere.

Since they had arrived, everything had been wonderful and spectacular. The gondola ride at the Venetian had proven to be especially charming—Quinn's old school friend, Brent Callahan, had been their gondolier. Brent had a spectacular tenor voice and he'd crooned love songs the entire way, pretending to be an Italian stranger, of course.

They'd even played craps for a while, and—she was proud to say—she'd been on fire! She'd rolled nicely, the table had been filled with cheers and laughter, and she and Quinn had managed to leave nicely ahead of the game.

You couldn't beat the cost of the trip, either. For years, Jeremy Anatoli, one of Quinn's oldest and dearest friends, and Brent's partner, had offered them a romantic getaway—or just a weekend away—whenever they wanted it. He was an executive host and assistant manager for the Excelsior, the very elegant casino hotel where they were staying. He had picked up their room, show tickets, anything else they might have desired.

The room he'd arranged for them was spectacular; the bed was mammoth and incredibly comfortable. It sat on a dais, heart-shaped with matching heart-shaped pillows. Floor to ceiling windows offered an amazing view of the strip. There was a full beautiful bathroom, and in addition, across from the bed, a heart-shaped whirlpool tub that helped fill out the "romantic" part, along with the champagne and strawberries that had awaited them.

"Ready to... gamble again, see a show, hit a club... ?" Quinn asked.

She grinned. "... go back to the room."

Quinn had the best slow smile. "I was hoping that might be your agenda, but, I thought I'd let you make the suggestion," Quinn said. "I mean, I've been trying to subtly suggest. A whisper in your ear here and there, my fingers dancing lightly down your spine... a little too far and all. But, as far as actually making the decision... "

She turned in his arms, came up on her toes, and kissed him on the lips. She meant for it to be a light kiss, a tender kiss. But, somewhere in the back of her mind, that word *suggestive* might have been lurking. Along with *sensual* and *seductive*. Their kiss deepened, became much more, tongues locking, steamy, liquid, and sweet, and for a moment, she forgot they were in public, the waters of the fountain bursting all around them. They broke apart and she blushed.

"Vacation in Vegas—no one even noticed!" Quinn assured her.

And it seemed they had not.

They turned. The Excelsior wasn't far. The streets were crowded, but not too much so. In an odd way, this area of Vegas was not unlike Bourbon Street—people were out in mass, happy, laughing, ready to leave their workaday world behind—and enjoy being wicked children. They passed the old and the young, the inebriated and the sober, crowds, couples, and loners.

Soon they were passing through the elegant cut-glass doors of the Excelsior. Greeters in handsome uniforms waved and smiled as they walked through entry—and, of course, straight into a massive sea of clinking, clanging, singing, and buzzing slot machines.

Quinn glanced down at Danni and shrugged. "Hey, this is the journey, not the destination."

She laughed. "Actually, I do like slot machines. The ones with great graphics. But…"

"On our way to a destination," he said.

Soft music, in stark contrast with the cacophony of the slot machines, played in the elevator. Their hallway was quiet. Quinn keyed the door open.

As yet, no one had closed the drapes. The room was in wonderful shadow with just a soft glow burning from a nightlight and the brilliant colors of the strip shining just beyond.

Danni started forward to pull the drapes; Quinn pulled her back into his arms. "No one can see in here," he assured her. "We're far, far above the crowd, enwrapped in the night."

"Ah, risqué!" she told him.

He kissed her. Quinn had such a way… his lips were forceful. Somehow they were damp and liquid and hot and entirely coercing. A kiss was never just a kiss… it went deeper, their mouths fused and not, tongues playing with intimacy and sweet suggestion.

She slipped her fingers beneath his jacket; he moved, never breaking the kiss, to let it fall to the floor. His fingers went to her waistband, her's to his belt buckle. Kissing and touching, laughing, whispering and teasing, they shed their clothing. In minutes, they had walked and stumbled to the bed. As they fell upon the ridiculously heart-shaped mattress, Danni wondered with awe how each time they touched it could feel so electrifying and new, and yet, still wonderfully perfect and comfortable. She marveled at the heat and feel of his muscled chest beneath her fingers, at the way he moved, at the sheer vitality of life in him and the way he touched her in return.

They'd probably both been thinking foreplay… and play. Maybe more of the champagne from the bottle in the bucket. A few slowly shared strawberries…

But maybe the fountains were *erotic* as well as romantic.

Maybe it was just the heart-shaped bed, or the play of colors beyond the windows. Maybe it was Vegas, with that wonderful touch of wicked.

They were quickly, almost frantically, wound together, limbs entwined, arching, writhing, feeling as if the neon lights that lit up the night beyond their shadows had burst within them. And, hot, damp, gasping for breath, they stared at one another and laughed. Danni rubbed the ball of her foot against his calf. "Okay, whirlpool tub now. Strawberries, um, tasting, licking, savoring… "

"Then you'd better move quickly," Quinn said. "That kind of pillow talk will get you pulled back into the covers again!"

Laughing, she leapt up. "Suds! I love suds. A huge whirlpool tub with suds everywhere, sleek, slippery, sensual…"

She froze a foot from the tub. She blinked.

They hadn't been alone in the room.

There was a man in their tub.

Not a voyeur, a thief, a masher… not a threat of any kind.

A dead man!

He lay in the empty tub, arms crossed over his chest, face contorted, mouth and eyes wide open, as if he had died of…

Fear. On his face a scream that could never now tear from his throat.

She didn't scream herself; she stood, stark naked and shivering fiercely, ice cold when she had been feeling so deliciously warm, staring at the whirlpool.

"Danni?" Quinn asked. "Is something wrong? What is it? What's the problem?"

She swallowed and turned and looked over at him where he lay, the shadows in the room all but hiding his face.

"Definitely something wrong, yes. We do have a problem. Quinn."

"What is it?"

He leapt out of bed, faster than should have been possible. "Danni…"

"There is a dead man in our bathtub."

And a one-eyed Jack had been tossed on top of his dead body.

*

Quinn knew that he and Danni had been through a lot—from the case of the Italian bust just after her father had died and on through many dangerous circumstances, the Hubert painting, the mysterious saxophone—and the dead they'd found in the bayou.

But, this was the first time that they'd found a dead man in their bathtub—in their room, not far from where they'd been making love. He knew that Danni was doing everything in her power to keep herself from screaming and shrieking and running from the room. Keeping calm as they called to report the situation. It wasn't that she

5

hadn't seen trouble or violence, or even dead people, before.

Just not in the tub where they should have been thinking of nothing but romance... and sex.

He was feeling a little on the very odd and somewhat violated side himself.

Not that it was the dead man's fault in any way.

"That's Harvey Sheen," Jeremy Anatoli said dully. "He's here often—he's what we call a Titanium guest—top of the top. He was a fairly famous magician when he was young and in England."

"A rich magician?" Randall asked.

Jeremy shrugged. "I guess he made enough to start investing. He did well in the stock market and kept investing and became a very rich man. He lost his wife a few years ago and I believe he's lonely. He loves playing, and he's never obnoxious. He talks with the cocktail waitresses and the croupiers and dealers, but just in a friendly way. He's a good guy. He *was* a good guy," he added sadly.

Jeremy was, of course, in their room now, along with a Detective William Parsons from the LVPD and his partner, Detective Jared Randall. Parsons was an older man who appeared as steady and weathered as the desert that surrounded the city. Randall was newer on the job, a tall, fit man with a shock of dark hair who seemed to know that he was the newbie; he did a lot of listening—and he still seemed quick to smile.

Parsons did not. He just looked worn and haggard.

A crime scene unit and the medical examiner were on the way.

Jeremy didn't own the hotel, but Quinn knew that their friend was truly a valued host; he was handsome and charming—and responsible to a fault. While the casino was extremely high end, it was still small as far as many of the enterprises in Vegas went—at the moment, as well as being an executive host, Jeremy was in charge. And the way that he looked at Quinn simply screamed "help!"

Danni stood behind the bed, by the windows that looked down at the strip. She was still and very quiet unless she was asked a question, regal and beautiful, even if her features were ashen. Danni had a swatch of auburn hair that curved around her face and shoulders and eyes that seemed as blue as the sky on a summer's day. He'd seen her ages before Angus had died, even if she hadn't known him; he'd always known she was a stunning young woman. She, too, was looking at Quinn and it was almost as if he could hear her words as well. "*See, we really should have gone off to a Caribbean island!*"

But, that Danni had come around and grasped her heritage so well wasn't something he'd always expected. And it wasn't a look of reproach that she was giving him, it was a look that seemed to say that she had expected this—that she had known something.

He didn't really want to be away from her, not now.

Then again, he'd fallen so impossibly in love with her that they often feared the depth of their relationship. They were partners, as well. It wasn't easy being madly in love with a partner—and afraid every time she made a move to solve a case. He'd learned to control himself.

Sometimes.

"So, you know this man," Parsons said to Jeremy. He looked at Quinn and Danni. "Do you know him?" he asked the two of them.

"No, I don't know him; I've never seen him," Quinn said. He expected Danni to say the same.

Naturally, in the few minutes it had taken after they'd thrown clothing on and called Jeremy and the police, Quinn had taken a look at the body. There was no discernible sign of trauma—but the man was more than obviously dead. Stone cold, eyes wide open, coloration changing. How the hell long had he been there? Quinn wasn't sure himself; he wished that they were home in NOLA where they knew the M.E., Dr. Hubert, and knew him well. They were in Vegas, where no one knew what they did, that he was a P.I., and that he and Danni were often working a consult with the police.

So much for vacation...

"I don't know him, but I did see him last night," Danni said.

"You did? Where?" Quinn was the one who asked, surprise evident in his voice.

"I saw him playing craps last night, right before Quinn and I went out," she said, addressing everyone in the room. "He came to the table soon after we finished playing."

"You have footage of the craps table, right?" Parsons asked.

Every casino had cameras everywhere; they had to have camera footage of their victim when he had played.

"Of course," Jeremy said. He looked over at Quinn, a bleak expression on his face. He sighed softly.

"We need to see all the footage," Randall said quietly.

"The M.E. and the crime scene folks... " Jeremy began.

"Are here," Parsons noted, stepping to the door; it was ajar. Hotel security officers were keeping a crowd from forming in the hallway. Everyone knew something had happened.

And everyone was curious. Whispers were already abounding.

The M.E. came in, a tall, lean, and quick man, immediately recognizable by his coat and his brisk manner; he headed straight to the corpse in the tub and asked, "Anyone touch the body?"

"No, Dr. Mac. Right?" he asked, looking at Quinn.

"Right," he said.

Quinn hadn't touched the body. He had taken note of the one-eyed Jack that lay on the man's chest. Danni had mentioned it right away. "*A one-eyed Jack,*" she had murmured.

"A one-eyed Jack mean anything in this casino?" Parsons asked.

"The usual—at cards, it means cheater" Jeremy said, looking desperately at Quinn and shaking his head. "Other than that... no. Not that I know about. Maybe it's just a cheater is a cheater"

"Randall, if you'll stay with Doc Mac, I'll head down and start looking at the footage," Parsons said.

"Sir, perhaps I should look at the footage with the casino host," Randall said, speaking up.

Parsons looked at him, frowning. Apparently, his younger partner didn't dispute him often.

Randall cleared his throat. "You had that eye surgery last month, sir."

Parsons didn't seem pleased. "Cleared for duty," he said briefly. "But, if that's your preference. Jeremy, if you would take Detective Randall to your surveillance, please, so that he may view that video?" He paused and turned and looked Quinn up and down. "I'll join you as soon as I'm done here."

"Mr. Quinn is with me," Jeremy said flatly. "He's here to consider being head of security."

That was a lie; Jeremy knew that Quinn couldn't leave NOLA for good.

Parsons shrugged.

Quinn looked over at Danni. She was still standing by the windows that looked over the neon lights and the beauty of the strip in all the color that beckoned and teased.

"If I'm allowed, I'll just step out, please," she said.

Quinn didn't want to have a conversation with Danni here and now—in front of these people. But, this was odd behavior for Danni. If he was heading out with Randall, he'd have thought that she'd stay here.

But, then, of course, they weren't home. They weren't on a case. They were on vacation. And it had been a wonderful vacation, filled with music, lights, fine food, and romance, and...

A dead man in the bathtub.

"I have your statement," Parsons told her gently. "You're free to go; of course, we need you to remain at the hotel. And, I'm sure, by some time tonight—or, I guess we're into today—you'll be able to come in and get your things. I am still curious, though. You say you were back in the room about half an hour or so before you even noticed that there was a man in the bathtub."

Quinn looked at Danni. Danni looked at Quinn.

"Ah, well, we were tired," Quinn said.

"Kind of just fell on the bed," Danni said.

Randall cleared his throat, smirking. "This is Vegas—fun and games for most people, Detective Parsons," he murmured softly.

"Oh. Oh! Yes, well, of course. Miss Cafferty, you're free to go. Randall, I'll be with you in the security booth when Doc has finished with our victim."

They still didn't even know what had killed the man! But, Danni seemed to have the urge to be somewhere else.

She looked at him and said, "I'll just be... I'll just be on the floor somewhere," she told him.

"Okay."

She came around the bed—skirting the giant tub and headed for the door without looking back at their dead man.

"You can come down the elevators with us," Randall told her. It looked as if he was going to take her arm to escort her. He looked at Quinn and apparently changed his mind. The four of them—Quinn, Jeremy, Detective Randall, and Danni—headed out of the room.

Once they were in the elevators, Randall glanced at Quinn. "You really never met the dead man before?"

"No."

"Why would someone leave him in your room?" Randall asked.

"I don't know. Large tub?" Quinn suggested.

"There shouldn't be that many keys out to a room like that," Randall noted.

9

Jeremy shook his head. "Plastic key cards," he said. "Our employees are all fingerprinted and vetted with serious background checks, but it doesn't take an Einstein to create a plastic key."

Quinn headed to the elevators, down to the main casino floor with its marble and columns, glitter and gold everywhere, and over to another elevator, following Detective Randall. Danni gave him a grim smile and nodded, turning toward the elegant playing floor.

He tried to worry about her. Danni, however, had that look about her that meant she was thinking about something, that she felt she was on some kind of a trail. She hadn't said anything to the police, nor to him, but, then again, she hadn't much chance to tell him anything.

The surveillance office at the casino was large. Glass windows—mirrored on the other side—ran the circumference of the area where Jeremy took them to run the video footage of the playing floor. Men and women, busy at their screens, nodded politely to them all; a floor boss directed who to watch where. Men and women occasionally asked for a second pair of eyes to watch a certain table.

Jeremy headed straight to the center console where a young man worked. He explained tersely what they needed; footage of which craps table and the time from the night before.

The man at the console backed the footage to the time requested. They watched in fast motion at first. Quinn saw himself and Danni playing at the one table. She was such fire! Alight and laughing, her hair swinging around her shoulders, her smiles for those around her pleasant, and the men and even the women at the table charmed by the fun she was having with her luck.

Harvey Sheen wasn't at the table when they were playing; Quinn saw that Harvey Sheen walked up just as he and Danni were leaving arm in arm.

In fact, Sheen brushed by Danni.

They watched as the man played craps; he laughed and joked with those around them. He wasn't a drinker; he turned down the cocktail waitress when she asked if he'd like something.

He liked to stand with his hands in his pockets.

"Go back," Quinn said suddenly.

The man at the controls did so. Quinn watched every move that Harvey Sheen made.

"That's it," he said softly.

"What's it?" Detective Randall asked.

"When he arrives, his hands are in his pockets. He jokes while he changes money—and when the dice come to him. Watch really carefully."

"I still don't see anything," Jeremy said, frowning as he looked at Quinn.

"The dice," Quinn told him. "Harvey Sheen is using his own dice. And someone saw him. That's why there was the one-eyed Jack with him in the whirlpool tub."

"No!" Jeremy protested. "I mean, we have these cameras going all the time. He's a regular here at the casino. I can't believe..." He stopped speaking suddenly, looking at Quinn. "We would have seen this by now, he can't be that good!"

"He was a magician—you told us so. Sleight of hand. He is good—so good that the cameras don't even pick up what he's doing," Quinn said.

"But you saw it right away." Jeremy groaned.

"Show me the video on the casino floor as he leaves, if you will," Detective Randall said. "He had to have been killed after he played. Someone at that table killed him. Maybe they lost a bundle."

"He wasn't losing a bundle—he was winning," Jeremy said flatly. He looked at Quinn. The way he looked at him, Quinn knew that they hadn't been pressed to come now out of friendship—Jeremy was worried about his casino and something had happened before tonight.

"Let's see where he went when he left, please," Randall said.

The man at the console began putting more images up on the screen.

They followed Harvey Sheen to the elevator. And then, suddenly, the screen went black.

"You've got to be kidding me," Detective Randall said.

"I'm doing everything I can, sir," the young man at the console said. "Gone—all the elevators just gone. The hallways, too!"

"How the hell?" Jeremy demanded.

"There's only one way—someone put a virus in the mainframe. We were hacked."

So Harvey Sheen's murder had been well planned. Hacking a casino computer system was almost impossible. He had played, and he had been placed in the whirlpool tub in their suite...

He turned to Jeremy. Jeremy was dead white.

"I was warned," he said softly, looking at Quinn, and not Randall.

"Warned?" Quinn asked.

Jeremy nodded. "I thought it was some kind of a joke. I accused Brent, even. Last week, when I got up to have my coffee, there was a playing card on my counter."

"You work at a casino," Randall said.

Jeremy nodded. "It was a one-eyed Jack. With a knife through the heart."

*

Danni headed straight back to the craps table where she had played before.

Where Harvey Sheen had played before he had died.

She tried to behave naturally; she played as she had played before. Of course, she wasn't laughing as much, and Quinn wasn't there and her romantic vacation—time away from the murder and mayhem and the extremely strange they faced in and through New Orleans events—was not proving to be idyllic. She kept trying to smile; to draw her fellow players into conversation. And she spoke to the pretty brunette croupier closest to her.

"You knew Harvey Sheen, right?" she asked the woman, whose name tag identified her as Barbara.

"Of course, I know Harvey," she said, and smiled, and Danni realized that, as of yet, no one else knew that Harvey was dead. "Such a great guy."

"Did everyone love him?"

"Oh, most people. Naturally, some of our other regulars were horribly jealous of him. He's a lucky dude—never walks away empty. The only thing is—and I'm always warning him—everyone knows he has money. I mean, I'd hate to see him rolled for that money!"

So, had he been killed for his money—and their tub was just a convenient place to leave his body?

That didn't seem right.

"There are people who think that Harvey has something magic. He was a magician, you know. Years and years and years ago. A famous magician. Did you want chips for that hundred?"

"Yes, yes, please," Danni said. She wasn't paying much attention to what she was doing. She kept seeing the one-eyed Jack.

Harvey had apparently had something—and those who watched closely enough might have seen something.

Envied and wanted that something.

"Harvey was a regular—were there other regulars playing with him tonight?"

Barbara looked at her suspiciously. "Why?"

"Winner!" another croupier called.

"Honey, you want to pick up your money?" Barbara asked. "Nice, honey! You just racked in a bundle there!"

Danni looked down and saw that her chips had grown; she hadn't actually picked them up—she'd left them all on the table. And now...

"Please," she whispered urgently to Barbara. "Was he playing with anyone else who is here regularly, who knew Harvey, knew about him being a magician?"

She looked at Danni and for a minute, Danni thought she was going to call security to come take her away. But then she frowned and said softly, "Max Cleary; he's a regular too. A wanna-be magician, of sorts. An entertainer, at any rate. He works a street show just outside. It's kind of a magic show. He plays in an Alice in Wonderland magic-show skit."

"Old, young—what does he look like?" Danni asked.

"Sixty-ish," Barbara said. "Tall, white hair. Good, strong face. Like an old western dude."

Danni thanked her and started to head away from the table.

"Your chips!" Barbara called.

Danni paused, then hurried back and scooped the chips into her purse.

Running a special place like the *Cheshire Cat* did require money! As she gathered up her chips, she asked, "What does he play?"

"Oh, he's one of the cards. The one-eyed Jack, I believe."

Danni froze; then she tore out into the street, digging her cell phone from her pocket as she did so.

*

The computer tech/security man at the console was still playing

13

with screens when Quinn glanced up to see on another screen that Danni was running toward the grand main entry to the casino. His phone rang just as he saw her head out the door.

"Watch her! Follow her!" he ordered, answering his phone.

It was Danni.

"Harvey Sheen had been a magician. He had something—"

"His own dice," Quinn said. "Danni, where are you going, what are you doing? Wait for me, wait for the cops—"

"I'm looking for a one-eyed Jack!" she told him.

Quinn ignored Randall and Jeremy and went running for the elevator. Randall followed after him—which turned out to be good, since he needed key codes to get back down to the street.

"What the hell?" Randall demanded.

"Danni thinks it's a one-eyed Jack," he said briefly.

"What? Harvey Sheen was killed by a card?"

"A man, of course, dressed as a giant one-eyed Jack," Quinn said.

The elevator arrived.

"Damn her—I told her we'd be right down. She's on the street, looking for street performers, and, she's supposedly waiting for us, but... "

*

It was late on the Vegas strip, but that didn't seem to stop any of the action. It was quieter, of course, than it had been earlier. There were people here and there—and no one-eyed Jacks.

She knew the name of the person she was chasing; he could be investigated when it was really morning.

No, Max Cleary would be gone after tonight. He'd watched Harvey Sheen constantly, and he had known his trick.

Special dice, according to Quinn. Fixed dice? Or magic dice?

A small alley ran around the casino to the endless valet parking in back. There was something on the ground on the path.

Compelled, she ran over to look. It was a one-eyed Jack.

She picked it up, held it and she remembered her dream. She remembered running and running—with a one-eyed Jack coming up hard on her.

Footsteps were coming her way; Quinn and the cops were

coming down, she knew. She turned, expecting them—and expecting too, that they'd lost the murderer.

It wasn't Quinn.

It had a head covered in some kind of red and black felt. It was a one-eyed Jack.

She couldn't head back to the street; no choice—Danni turned and fled into the alley.

And the one-eyed Jack bore down close behind her.

An eerie laughter seemed to come in her wake as well, swirling on the air, teasing—and menacing.

"Stop, stop! You don't understand. I didn't do it! I swear to you, I didn't do it!"

Danni fled, hard and fast. She raced through cars. She could see the valet area, men working, people, all she had to do was reach...

"Stop!"

He was close! The giant one-eyed Jack chasing her was almost on her.

She saw a door—and she grabbed it. An employee entrance. She prayed it wasn't locked; it wasn't.

But, it was so late! She burst into a hallway—with no one. She tried to slam the door—he was there; he was right behind her.

She kept running and burst into a large room. A costume room—it was filled with supplies for the various shows put on at the casino, sequins and features, rows and rows of costumes...

She ran through them.

And the one-eyed Jack was there.

"I don't know who you are, miss! I don't know why you think that I did this! Everyone will think that I did this. It wasn't me. I swear it. But, I do think that I know who did! Please, please, listen to me."

*

Quinn burst out into the street; it was quiet. He looked both ways.

Danni had vanished.

"Where the hell is she?" Randall demanded, panting as he came to a halt at Quinn's side.

Quinn headed to the left, to the right... he had a good view down

15

the strip. No sign of Danni anywhere. And she'd said that she'd wait, but...

Something caught his eye. Something on the ground.

A one-eyed Jack. It lay right before the narrow alley stretched that led around the casino and separated it from the next behemoth.

He ran that way; Randall came after him.

*

Danni didn't believe that she was sitting in a pile of feathers on an employee sofa in the bowels of the casino, talking to a one-eyed Jack.

She believed him; she couldn't help but believe.

"I have to let Quinn know!" she exclaimed suddenly, reaching for her phone. "Oh, my God, I have to tell him right away!"

"Danni!"

She heard her name called. She was about to answer, but Max Cleary clamped a hand over her mouth. "The costumes, get behind the costumes."

"It's Quinn!"

"But, he might not be alone."

And he wasn't; she heard Detective Randall calling her name as well.

They both leapt up; Max Cleary caught a hold of her arm and pulled her along with him. They dodged behind a mannequin in a giant headdress, and then down, down into a pile of satin and silk, sequins and glitter. Raw materials for the seamstresses who worked the entertainment area.

"They in here?" she heard Randall ask.

"You take the hall," Quinn said.

"Wait—what's that?" Randall demanded. "Something moved."

He was coming toward them—coming right toward Max Cleary and Danni.

Max suddenly pushed her up—and threw a pile of coins across the room. "Go!" he whispered urgently to her.

"They're here!" Randall swore.

Danni ran, into the hall—and then into the next room. It was a dressing room; rows of tables with makeup were aligned along both walls. It wasn't just any dressing room—it was a dressing room for clowns! There were rows of costumes, mannequins with half-sewn costumes, masks, wigs, and more.

She looked around for a trunk, a closet, anywhere to go.

And then, she heard the door burst open and scurried to the back, ducking under one of the tables.

Then nothing.

Footsteps.

And then...

"I know you're in here, Miss Cafferty. And I know that you know who killed Harvey Sheen. You just had to go after Max tonight. Had you just waited... by morning, I would have hidden the dice. He had magic dice, you see, Miss Cafferty. Magic! He could call any number, and it would come up. Illegal, of course, but Harvey Sheen, well, he played it to the bone. I've watched him. Okay, to be honest, I went through the academy, I've spent a year working with that wretched old geezer, Parsons, just to manage this. Timing had to be perfect. I had to investigate the casino—only way to get close. Oh, I have bided my time. I took computer classes, casino classes—I worked so damned hard. Now, if you hadn't come out the way you did, old Max Cleary would have had no idea. Now, you see, he knows that I did it—because I was afraid that he'd been watching me. Just as I watched him. Perfect patsy. And, hey, who questions one of the police's finest when he's always around the casino? I'm so sorry—I have to kill you quickly and then find Max and kill him, and well, then, you know how it goes."

He was coming closer and closer. There was no way to run. And even if Quinn reached her, he wouldn't know. Detective Randall would just turn and...

Shoot Quinn.

She could see Randall's feet. Each step brought him nearer.

"Hey!"

To her amazement, right when the feet reached her, one of the clown mannequins suddenly moved and talked.

"Hey, buddy boy, over here!" the clown said.

It started to move; to race deeper into the room.

A shot was fired.

Then, the door burst open.

And Quinn was there.

"Quinn, stop, be careful—!"

"I've found the killer!" Detective Randall said. He was going to turn and fire.

Fire at Quinn.

Danni leapt out, throwing herself at the detective. Her impetus knocked them both to the floor, but Randall was quick and strong and he quickly wrangled her down beneath him, reaching for his gun.

"I wouldn't."

The words were spoken harshly in Quinn's deep, rich voice. He was standing next to them then.

"You can shoot me, but I can get that gun. And I'll shoot and kill your precious Miss Cafferty," Randall said, almost smiling. His hands were on his gun.

"Oh, no, I don't think so. I've been around a while. I am a dead aim and you know the saying—faster than a speeding bullet."

Was it bravado? Randall had his gun; she'd stopped him from shooting Quinn, but he had the gun in his hands.

"But, you love her," Randall reminded him.

"More than life itself," Quinn agreed. "Let her up."

Danni watched as emotions ripped through Detective Randall's eyes. He was desperate. He was caught. He'd worked hard and long and...

Maybe it was worth killing her, since she'd somehow ruined it all for him.

"Hey!"

Suddenly, Max Cleary—now half one-eyed Jack and half clown—suddenly jumped out from the costume area.

"You can't shoot anything!" he said to Detective Randall.

"What?"

Danni looked, just as Randall looked.

He was no longer holding a gun.

He was holding a card. A giant one-eyed Jack.

Randall screamed and dropped the card; it was suddenly a gun again. He grasped Danni by the throat in a rage, but Quinn was there, ripping the man from her, tossing him halfway across the room. He pulled Danni to her feet, kicking the gun far back, and he turned for Randall, but it wasn't necessary.

Detective Parsons, worn and weary, had arrived, and while she, Quinn and Max Cleary all shouted, trying to warn Parsons about the truth, the man just reached down for his partner.

"Thank God!" Randall began.

"You're under arrest," Parsons said flatly.

Uniformed officers burst into the room, ready to take Randall away.

"Never did like that upstart for a partner," Parsons said simply. "Just never did cotton to the guy—had a wiseass mouth on him and no respect for his elders. Mr. Cleary!" he said then. "I get the feeling you were one hell of a magician yourself."

"I think you'll find Harvey Sheen's magic dice in Detective Randall's pocket," Danni said, no longer trembling as she stood securely with Quinn; his arm rested around her shoulder.

"Mr. Randall, Miss Cafferty. Randall here is no longer a member of LVPD."

*

"I admit, I called you and begged and insisted because of the card I found on the counter," Jeremy said. "I mean, I didn't even know why I should be scared then, but, I was. I needed you guys out here."

"Why didn't you tell us right away?" Quinn asked.

They were at the rooftop restaurant.

And Danni was glad, glad of the beauty, glad to be with such good friends. And Vegas suddenly seemed fun—wickedly fun as well.

From where they sat, everything was beautiful. The sky seemed alive with color, all of the Vegas lights celebrating as if they were magical themselves, illuminating the night beyond the picture windows.

"He thought I did it at first!" Brent said indignantly, before sipping from his champagne glass. "But, I don't play tricks."

"And I knew that. I really knew that," Jeremy said.

"Okay, so Randall was a detective frequently called when there was an incident at the casino," Danni said. "So, he could fix the cameras, he had easy access—and he obviously planned all along that it would be blamed on Max Cleary—another magician, a guy who was always playing craps with Harvey and knew him well. But... "

"But why the hell did he put the man in our whirlpool?" Quinn demanded.

Jeremy sighed. "I guess because I'd told him that I had special guests coming. And he knew that you were a P.I. in Louisiana. That

19

way, when he did manage to kill Cleary, you would have been a witness. Cleary would have run—and Randall would have shot him. It would have all appeared to above board—a good shoot. A clean shoot—a killer would have been escaping."

"What he didn't count on," Brent said, grinning at her, "was Danni. Danni having the whatever to head straight to the craps table, finding out about Max Cleary right away."

"And he didn't count on Max," Danni said.

"How did he turn the gun into a giant card?" Quinn demanded.

"I don't know, the cops don't know—no one knows," Jeremy told them. He lifted his hands. "Magic," he said.

Their dinner went on. They managed to talk about others things, to catch up.

And despite everything, it was wonderful to be with friends.

"Of course," Jeremy told them, when the meal had ended, "we have a new room for you. It's the penthouse. I think you'll like it."

He and Brent took them to their new room. It was even better than the first.

The whirlpool was out on the balcony.

The balcony was locked.

Jeremy hugged them both and gave them the keys. Before he left, he reached into his pocket. "These are the dice. The magic dice. Maybe they're just loaded dice. I don't know. But, I think they need to go home with you—and be kept in a special basement in New Orleans."

Quinn nodded and took the dice.

Danni hugged Jeremy and Brent, too. They left them.

And the minute they were gone, she turned into Quinn's arms.

They kissed, shedding their clothing. Laughing, awkward, elegant, and falling upon the new bed.

Then, for a moment, they just held one another; the room didn't matter. Nothing mattered. Except for the two of them. They made love, and made love again.

As another moon shone benignly down on the glitter of night, they lay together.

"I was just thinking," Quinn said.

"What?"

"This is magic. You and me together. That's real magic."

She couldn't agree more.

2

THE COUNTESS AND THE PILOT

Lance Taubold & Richard Devin

The Countess Greta sauntered through the new Excelsior hotel. To others she appeared nonchalant, regal, a woman of confidence, yet inside she was nearly overcome with a feeling making her feel totally bereft. Her silk, floor-length cape was satin lined and trimmed in the richest of white ermine. She sashayed as she walked; the cape mimicking her in counter rhythm. The hotel guests of the Excelsior cast furtive glances her way. One could perfectly read the wonderment on their faces as they pondered who this curious beauty could be, and more... what her story was.

*

Moments later, she stood gazing out the floor-to-ceiling windows of her suite. She had been here for three months, living a quiet existence in her suite of rooms that occupied a quarter of the twentieth floor of nearly the tallest building in the city—overlooking the burgeoning Las Vegas Boulevard. Much of her view beyond the Strip was of barren desert. She turned her gaze from the lights of the casinos toward the vast emptiness of the desert and allowed her thoughts to slip back into time and to relive her life and the fortunes and misfortunes that filled it.

Her ex-husband had provided her with the means to escape Europe, the Nazis, and a life that would surely have been short-lived had he not sacrificed for her. Hermann had been handsome and strong and so entrenched with Hitler and his nefarious Third Reich that leaving for him was impossible. Instead, he had allied with Himmler, becoming a confidant of the Nazi leader, but all along they had been secretly negotiating with the Allies. Shortly before the imminent end of the war, Hitler suspected Hermann's treason and had him executed.

Hermann had been prepared for this day and already had secreted away a veritable fortune. The evening before his execution, while she was allowed to visit him, he had told her where the money was hidden.

After Hermann was killed, the days became a flurry of madness and confusion. She laughed a sad little laugh as she recalled reading that Hitler had committed suicide in the Eagle's Nest two days later—a mere two days—if only... and her husband would be alive. But fate had seen things differently. And her husband was gone— seven days before their daughter was born.

She could not stay in Germany. Her husband had aided the Allies and helped bring the war to an end much quicker, but he had made enemies in doing so. She had to take her daughter and escape.

America.

She would change her identity, become a countess. Someone mysterious, who would not be asked questions... only talked about. Royalty was often above suspicion. The perfect cover.

But again fate stepped in. Hermann's good friend Martin Bormann came to her, offering passage to South America. She took it.

It was ten long years in Argentina spent with those Nazis who made it out of Germany and took refuge in Argentina. But she had not been a Nazi. She had hated Hitler and all he had done. The murders. The atrocities. She spent much of the time as far away from the others as possible. She hated those who sympathized with the Nazis. So she bided her time until the opportunity arose to travel to America.

An older, benevolent American named Jeffrey James had been visiting Buenos Aires and by chance had struck up a friendship with her. After several revealing conversations, she came to trust him, and he her, ultimately telling him her sordid tale—most of it anyway. He took Greta and her daughter under his wing and offered to take her back with him as his wife—in name only. It turned out that Jeffrey was interested in other gentlemen, and he needed a confidant as much as she did. She would be the perfect cover for him to continue his life in Hollywood, California.

Greta had accepted, and at thirty-five with her ten-year-old daughter, they moved to America, settling in the hills of Hollywood among the famous and infamous. She found herself quite at peace there. Life was pleasant and Jeffrey treated her and her daughter very well. All of his friends loved the exoticism of his being married to a countess. He produced films and seemed to know everyone in Hollywood.

Then fate stepped in once again. On a particularly spectacular night, warm and star-filled, driving through Malibu, a drunk driver hit Jeffrey head-on. The police said he was killed instantly. Greta was a widow for the second time. Now she had even more wealth. She could stay content in the large, comfortable house that Jeffrey had built for them, but Hollywood was still foreign to her, and most of their friends had really been Jeffrey's friends. She needed to move on. Her daughter went east to New York for her education and was developing her own life there.

Several months before, Jeffrey and Greta had been invited to Las Vegas for the opening of a new hotel, the Excelsior. She had loved the experience and the energy in Vegas. Jeffrey had known the owner of the Excelsior, Louis "The Lip" LaFica, and despite his somewhat tainted ties to the Mafia, she had enjoyed his company—perhaps because they were both hiding something. Louis had offered an open invitation to her as his personal guest whenever she wished to stay in Vegas.

She contacted Louis... and here she was.

She enjoyed the nightlife and the entertainers—many of which she'd met through Jeffrey in Hollywood. She gambled occasionally, which was a fun diversion for a while. But she was missing something. Or more precisely *someone*. Someone to share life with. She wondered where or if there was the man who could understand her... or forgive her?

*

Trevor Marsh had had too much drink. *Way* too much. His boss had told him to charge whatever he wanted. He had. And now he was regretting it.

At least he didn't have to fly tomorrow. He had a few days in Las Vegas before Mr. Hughes needed to return. Of course, if he'd had to fly, he would never have had anything to drink... at least not this much. His boss put him up at the Excelsior. It was beautiful, filled with so many classy people. He thought he'd spotted Dean Martin earlier across the bar. And he was *sure* he'd just seen Marlene Dietrich, or maybe her younger sister. Did Marlene have a sister? It didn't matter, this woman was stunning! The most beautiful woman he'd ever seen. A long, pink dress that clung to every inch of that luscious body. She had to be a movie star. He felt drawn to her. He should talk to her. But she would probably laugh at him. Who was he? An ex-air force pilot, flying a private plane for some eccentric rich guy. A failed marriage. A lot of regrets. Germany... Korea... No. He didn't need to go there. Too much pain. Too many deaths.

He got up from the barstool... and immediately fell to the ground. A man at a nearby stool rushed over to him. "Hey, you all right?"

"Yeah, I'm fine," he managed to get out. "Just tripped. I'm fine."

"Okay." The man took note of Trevor's uniform. "You fly?"

"Yeah."

"I hope not soon."

"Got a frew... few days off. I'm going to go to my room."

"Good idea. Good luck."

As he steadied himself with a grip on the edge of the bar, Trevor caught the reflection of his vision of loveliness going around a corner of the casino. He started to stagger after her. He had to meet her.

He went around the corner and... there she was. Well, a part of her. He caught sight of the flowing cape as it disappeared into the elevator. He lurched toward the closing door and... fell once again.

24

This time there was no one to see him. He looked up at the elevator panel and noted the floors as it ascended. He lay there watching the numbers: 16... 17... 18... 19... 20! It stopped. She was on the twentieth floor. But which room?

He pushed himself up and lunged for the elevator button.

"Come on. Come on."

Ping. The elevator doors opened. Empty. He got in and hit twenty.

Adrenaline pumped through him. He rested his head against the door and closed his eyes as the elevator chimed away the floors.

Mistake.

The door opened. And for a third time, Trevor found his face kissing the floor.

"Ow! This is getting ridico—dicle—oh shit!"

He braced against the wall and struggled up, certain he was going to be hurting in the morning. He had made it. Now where was she? His eyes tried to focus on the numbers adorning each of the double-wide doors. There weren't many of them. "Must be all big suites. Maybe I should knock." He raised a fist to a door. "Maybe not. Can't get found out; the boss would be pissed."

He stumbled to the next door. Unable to get his legs and feet to cooperate with walking, he fell back against it.

The door opened.

This time he fell backward.

Crack!

He hit his head hard on the marble entryway.

Blackness.

*

Who was he? Greta stared at the handsome face. The man was out cold. But he was breathing at least. He had close-cropped dirty-blond hair, a square powerful jaw, aquiline nose, and a solid physique. Early forties? He wore a blue—she guessed—pilot's uniform, collar opened, white crew-necked T-shirt showing.

She guessed he had Nordic or Germanic heritage, and he could have been the brother to her deceased husband Hermann. She clutched her throat at the thought. In the supine position, she estimated his height at six feet. There wasn't a sign of bleeding. No blood spilling out from the back of his head. At least he hadn't cracked his head open.

The entryway was all marble and she contemplated dragging him most of the way to the living room. She could call for assistance, she supposed. But then there would be explanations and gossip. Something she wished to avoid. She stepped around the man, took hold of both feet, and pulled.

She managed to get him to the sofa and propped him up along the front. If she could only rouse him for a moment, perhaps with his help she could get him onto the sofa. She put one of his arms up and tried to tug on him. She heard a grunt. His head hit her breast and she momentarily flinched at the sensation—not altogether unpleasant. It had been so long...

"Help me get you up," she said pulling on both arms now. "I'll get you on the couch, just help me." With some effort, and him in a semi-conscious state, she managed to get him to his feet. His head moved between her breasts and he groaned. She enjoyed the frisson of excitement that his hot breath on her breasts released in her.

Miraculously, he scooted himself up... and passed out, this time falling back onto the soft cushions of the sofa.

"That was not so difficult, my handsome man. I will get you a blanket." She received a loud snore in response. "What am I doing?" she questioned herself out loud. Then without another thought, removed his shoes, loosened his belt and the top button on his trousers, and began to unbutton his shirt. Her hands froze at the first button, then at each of the remaining buttons as she undid each. Through his T-shirt she could see the strong muscles of his chest and the flat stomach beneath it. She had the urge to run her hands over him. *Why not? He is clearly passed out. It would not be proper, but who would know.* She reached out a tentative hand. His chest was warm, almost hot to her touch. Or maybe it was her? Two incredibly taut mounds of muscle. She lay her hands on him. She drew in a quick breath. *God save me.* She had not felt this rush of warmth in a very long time— possibly never. She closed her eyes and basked in the sensuality of her act. Her body tingled everywhere. She wanted more.

She got it.

In the next moment, she was engulfed in his arms, his lips covering hers.

She didn't resist.

His mouth opened and his tongue connected with hers. She felt a jolt in every nerve in her body. This couldn't be happening. She made a half-hearted attempt to push away. He pulled her in closer and kissed her even more deeply. She gave in. More than gave in. She ravished his mouth as he ravished hers. Her hands tore at his chest, seemingly not able to grab him hard enough. She needed more. Her hands went up under his T-shirt. And as soon as they touched the bare flesh, she was lost. She caressed, squeezed, clutched the hard flesh of his pectorals, pinched the taut nipples. Her hands moved to his waist and... he went still. His lips stopped moving. His body stopped writhing with her touch. He had passed out again.

Rational thought came back to her slowly. What had she just done? It was insane! She needed some air—or maybe a brandy. *Yes. A brandy.*

She moved to the bar and poured two fingers into a crystal snifter. Her hands shook as she took a long swallow. Then sauntered back to the sofa, feeling more in control.

She looked down at man passed out on the sofa. "Who are you?"

Eyelids fluttered. He stared up at her saying, "Are you an angel? Am I in heaven?"

She smiled, despite herself and the situation, and felt a warm glow at the question. "No," was all she could say.

"But you're so beautiful." He closed his eyes and began breathing deeply.

"And you are so handsome, my mysterious stranger." Her eyes misted as she took another sip of the brandy, covered the stranger with a blanket, and then sat next to the sofa in an overstuffed side chair. She downed the last bit of brandy and slipped into sleep.

She was roused by a deep, strong voice.

"Where am I?"

She opened her eyes and took a moment to realize she had fallen asleep in the plush chair. Her empty snifter sat on the brass and glass coffee table. She tried to formulate a proper response. "You had, uh, a slight accident. I helped you into my suite and, uh... "

He tried to sit up. "Ohhh, my head is killing me." He lay back.

"Yes, I believe you hit it quite hard when you fell."

"Where am I?" He put a hand to his forehead. "Wait. I was in the casino... drinking... I was following... *You!*"

"You were following me?" A slight bit of concern slipped into her voice.

He blushed. "I... well... Hell!... I was drinking!"

"Yes, that was evident."

He blushed again.

She found it charming.

"You have a name?"

"Oh, Jesus, I'm sorry." He sat up, blinking hard. "I'm not usually rude like this, but... you gotta believe me this isn't like me. I was feeling bad, and I have a few days off, and the drinks were free, and you were there, and—"

She fought back a smile—not very successfully—"You were telling me your name?"

"Oh, sorry. Trevor; it's Trevor, Trevor Marsh. I'm a pilot. Private pilot. I used to fly for TWA. Korea before that. Germany before that. St. Louis born and bred."

"I'm the Countess Greta." She paused, realizing how officious she sounded, at least to her own ears. "Greta, please, you may call me Greta."

"Oh my God! A countess! You're a countess?" He started to rise, then fell back.

She laughed. "Please, don't stand. I appreciate the attempt, however."

"I feel like an ass."

"These things happen. My deceased husband tied on quite a few while we were married," she said, recalling the many evenings of debauched drinking at one Hollywood soiree or another.

"I'm sorry. You're widowed? That was stupid. Of course you're widowed. You just said 'deceased.'"

She found herself laughing again.

"What a beautiful laugh you have," he said, smiling.

"Thank you. It seems as if I haven't laughed for so long."

"You should. It's delightful."

"Thank you." Now she felt herself blushing.

They stared at each other.

"I didn't mean to embarrass you."

"No, it's..."

He helped her, "So, what exactly happened? How did I get here? I remember being in that bar in the center of the casino. And I saw you and thought you were Marlene Dietrich or some big Hollywood star. I knew you had to be because you're so beautiful... " He paused for a moment, looking into her eyes. "I think I followed you... well I must have, because I'm here. I just don't remember much else. Wait. Did I... ?"

She couldn't meet his gaze.

"I kissed you," he said, almost with reverence.

She didn't respond. She couldn't.

"I am *so* sorry. I've never done anything like that in my life! I can't believe you didn't have me thrown out... or *arrested!*"

She noticed him pale at his last statement. "I would never have had you arrested. Please, you needn't worry on that account."

He relaxed and eased back. "I need my job. Since my wife left me, things have been hard. She kept saying I was cheating on her whenever I was away flying. The truth: *she* was the one having the affair with a friend of mine. Then one day, my flight was cancelled, and just like in a movie, I went home and walked in... and the rest is history. Well, except the part where Mr. Hughes needed a private pilot because his own had shown up drunk one day. What an idiot. Fired on the spot. And there I was fresh from a flight, and since he owns TWA, I was ready, willing, and able. He said he'd heard good things about me, knew I flew in WWII and Korea, and would I be willing to take him and his guest—coincidentally enough—to good old Las Vegas. So, here I am. He's got business here for a few days. And he brought his newest girlfriend, Gail Ganley. She was that actress in that movie *Blood of Dracula*—not a bad movie—and so I'm free as a bird. And thank God for that. If he'd seen me like this... You are an angel—my guardian angel. You saved me."

Greta had no response. An angel? Not her. Not ever. What would he say if he knew who she really was? She said, "So you flew in both wars?"

"Yes ma'am," he said. Germany and Korea. His face was grim. The Nazis, the Japs. Man's inhumanity to man. Only worse. We knew what was going on, and we waited, so long we waited. If only Hitler had taken himself out sooner... "

"Yes, sooner," she found herself saying.

"Did I just make the biggest faux pas ever? You're German aren't you? I'm sorry, I didn't mean to offend you."

"It's quite all right, believe me. I quite agree. Many of us opposed Hitler, my husband..." She stopped herself. What was she doing? She couldn't tell him. This stranger. This *handsome* stranger. She stood. "I am going to get you some ice for your head. I am sure it is aching. You hit it quite hard when you fell."

"I fell?"

"Yes." She gave a slight smile, remembering his inauspicious entrance. "I heard some commotion in the hall; I went to the door and opened it. Apparently, you were leaning against it with your back. When I opened the door, you fell backward and cracked your head rather soundly on the floor."

He gave her an odd look. "And how did I wind up on your couch—comfy as it is?"

"Well... I dragged you across the marble, and when I got you to the sofa, you woke for a moment and helped me get you onto it." She hoped she wasn't blushing again.

"Wow. That was above and beyond the call of duty, Greta." He paused, as if unsure to continue. "And then to thank you... I kissed you. What a heel I am."

Thinking about that kiss, she turned her back, afraid that her smile would betray her, "I will get your ice."

*

Trevor lay there. Thoughts spun through his mind. Questions: How had he gotten himself into this? Drunk? Kissing a beautiful countess? It was crazy. It was like a strange, yet wonderful, dream. A dream he never wanted to wake up from. He thought about the kiss and how, even in his drunken state, that kiss surged through him. His desire grew and stirred in his loins. He hoped to get another chance—this time sober.

"Here is the ice." She placed the improvised ice bag behind his head. With her other hand, she brushed the hair back from his forehead.

He noticed that she let her hand linger, fingers gently touching his hair. It felt like a caress. He closed his eyes and enjoyed the simple touch.

"You don't have a fever," she said.

"That feels wonderful."

She pulled her hand away.

His eyes flew open. "The ice, I meant. Sorry."

She stared at him.

So beautiful. Smiling, he couldn't resist adding, "But your hand felt wonderful too." *I made her blush again.* "Why didn't you call house security to help you?"

She remained silent, and then the words came in a flurry. "I... I'm not sure. I did not want to bother them. There was no blood; you were breathing and... and... I don't know."

He gave a small laugh. Then he made a decision. This might be his last chance. He needed to go for it. "Would you talk to me for a while? Tell me about yourself?"

She stared at him, then said, "Trevor." She motioned to him to give her a space on the sofa. She sat next to him, their bodies touching. "Before I tell you about myself, I would like to hear a little more about your life."

"What would like to know? I'll tell you everything."

She didn't expect quite so honest a response. "I noticed a haunted look come into your eyes when you spoke of your time in Korea, and especially Germany."

He stared at her for a moment before he began. "If I could go back and do it all again, I wouldn't. It was my duty as a pilot and an American, but I regret it. Every day that I had to fly and fight, and bomb cities and villages, made me want to be the one that got shot down. We were all just boys really. We went right from our schools and families into war. We did what we were told and had no time for questions. We were taught to hate the enemy. We were as bad as the Jerrys that way. Everyone was the enemy." He swallowed hard and continued. "I took their lives. They would never *have* lives because of me. After the war ended, and everyone was so exuberant and happy, I couldn't be. What we had done haunted me. All those lost lives. I tried to get a job then, but there was nothing. Nothing for a kid whose only talents were flying a plane and killing people. So, I went back in. The Air Force was the only thing I knew. The only place I felt I belonged. I was lost. I was moody and sullen. No one understood me.

"Korea wasn't any better. The only difference was the shape of their eyes. I was older, but certainly not wiser. The only thing the years had taught me was how to make myself numb. I closed off all feelings and did the job. After I got out, I heard TWA airlines was looking for pilots, and I applied. It was something I could do... and not kill anyone. I flew for them for a couple of years, met my wife, who was a stewardess for the airline; we got married. A year ago I walked in on her with one of my fellow pilots. We fought. Got divorced. Met Mr. Hughes... and here I am." He paused as he gazed directly into her eyes, "Here I am with the most beautiful woman I've ever met."

Greta pulled a handkerchief from her cape and dabbed at her eyes. *This man was extraordinary.*

"I didn't mean to make you cry." He took her hand.

She felt the warmth and strength issuing from his grip. "You are an amazing man, and forgive me for saying your wife was a fool."

"Thank you for saying that. For a long time, I thought I was the fool. That means a lot to me."

She squeezed his hand back.

Their eyes met again.

Then their lips.

She fell into his arms, gave in to his soft lips and masculine scent. Their tongues joining. Her hands drawn to his muscular chest, probing and squeezing. He felt so good. So male. She slid her hand under his T-shirt, needing to feel his raw flesh. This time, however, he was sober and more accommodating. He stripped his shirt off.

She drew back to gaze at his nakedness. Exquisite. Taut muscles, chiseled as if by Michelangelo. He blushed at her blatant stare, then slid his own hands up her arms and brushed them with his fingertips. He slipped his fingers beneath the strap of her gown and lowered it. Her breasts fell free.

Now he gazed at *her.* His sharp intake of breath let her know she pleased him. His hands, ever so slowly, moved beneath her breasts and cupped them.

"Glorious," he said with reverence.

She gave a quiver and released a soft moan.

Slowly, he began to knead and caress the delicate mounds of flesh. She leaned forward and braced her hands on his chest. His thumbs brushed over her nipples and began to rotate on them rhythmically.

She clutched his chest in response, a louder moan this time.

He moved his hands to her sides, scorching her, and brought her body into him. He took a nipple into his mouth and stroked it with tongue, suckled it with his lips. She felt the sensation deep in her womanhood, and she wriggled her hips on his. She was completely his. She didn't want him to stop the incredible things he was doing to her breasts, but she wanted more. She pulled back, her nipple making a soft *pop* when it escaped his mouth, causing her to make a quick intake of breath. The cool air, after his hot mouth, made her nipple even more erect. Her hands lowered to his belt and she frantically undid it.

She looked down. He was exposed and large... and ready for her.

He slid his hands up her thighs, under her dress, and in a split second, she was as naked as he was.

Their bare flesh connected explosively in raw, anguishing heat.

She reached down and grabbed him in her hand. He gasped loudly, as if he'd been burned by her touch. She loved the feel of him, of being barely able to get her hand around him. She wanted him inside her.

Now.

She guided him into her wetness. She was more than ready for him. As soon as she had him at her entrance, she thrust down, taking him all the way inside her. She cried out at the pain and overwhelming pleasure. Pleasure she thought impossible. Pleasure she thought she would die from.

She heard his cry at the same time as hers, not caring if she'd been too quick or violent. He began thrusting up into her, hard. Pounding her. She met his pounding with her own downward thrusting. Her hands on his chest, clutching and clawing. His hands on *her* breasts, kneading and tugging.

The tension was building. If she didn't release soon, she would explode.

His grunting and groaning matched hers.

She knew he was as frantic for climax as she was.

Harder now. Faster. The wave crested. He grabbed her and pulled her lips to his, devouring her.

They cried out in unison.

Oblivion.

She woke. Warm arms were around her, holding her, massaging her naked back. She felt warm breath at her temple and ear. Butterfly kisses.

"Are you back with me?" he murmured.

"Yes," she whispered.

"Do you always do that?"

She could hear the humor in his voice, while he nuzzled her neck. "Never," she admitted.

Now she could feel him smiling against her cheek. "Good. I want to be the only one."

Tears came to her eyes. Those might be the sweetest words she'd ever heard.

"May I say something to you?" Her breasts were bared to him; her face was bared to him. And also her heart. "I don't care if what you did you felt was wrong or inappropriate. I don't care about your past, who you are or were. There was a reason you walked by my drunken self in the casino. I was supposed to meet you. We are supposed to be together... "

She wanted him to stop as much as she wanted him to continue.

His hands came up and he held her face, directed at his own. "I love you, Greta. I love you. I *know* as sure as I'm lying here, that you're the reason for me to keep going on with my life. You've made me feel something again."

He brought her face down to his and kissed her so tenderly that she thought her heart would break.

She didn't want time to continue.

The kiss broke, and reality and guilt swept in.

"Before anything else is said—"

"You don't have to tell me anything, Greta."

She took in a deep breath before revealing the words she had feared to utter before. "I am not a countess. I was born in Germany, the youngest of three girls. My real name is Gretl not Greta. In my teens, I was surrounded by the Nazis. They were everywhere. My oldest sister was in love with a Jew, a wonderful man that my family adored. I feared for his life and hers. They escaped the country just as the worst of it began. I believe my other sister may have helped them, but she never spoke of it, and I have not heard from her or her husband since. I can only hope that they made it out and are living a good life. I was married to a man who was close to Hitler and his inner circle. Hermann Fegelein was his name. It was close to the end of the war and my husband was working with Himmler and the Allies, both of them knowing the war was lost and trying to bring it to an end as quickly as possible."

She tried to read Trevor's face, but his look was inscrutable. "I was pregnant and nearing the end of my term. Hitler discovered the plot with the allies and Hermann's involvement with it. He sentenced my husband to be executed. My husband was executed the next day, and two days after that... Hitler killed himself.

"Our daughter was born five days after that. Unbeknownst to me, my husband had been secreting away money in preparation for our escape. Before he died, he told me where he had hidden it. A short time after, with the help of friends, I and my daughter escaped to South America, Argentina, and for the next several years I remained there, hiding in plain sight as a countess from Europe.

"Then I met Jeffrey, a movie producer from Hollywood, California. He was a homosexual. He would have been killed had he lived in Germany. He thought that we could be of use to one another. We would be married. I would go to America, where he would have his cover of a wife and be free to live his life without the scandal of people trying to expose him, and I would be free to do as I wished. Jeffrey was very good to us and it was an agreeable situation. He was killed in an automobile collision and I was again widowed and alone. My daughter was going to school in the east. I had all the money I would ever need. I had been to Las Vegas several times with Jeffrey, and one time with your boss, Mr. Hughes, I might add."

She stopped her narrative for a moment, noting the puzzled reaction from her mentioning Hughes. "Jeffrey was completely fine with me doing as I pleased and encouraged me to go. And as it was a quick flight to Vegas, I went on one of Mr. Hughes' private planes. I saw it as more of a way to break the boredom of Hollywood, but Mr. Hughes, I'm afraid, had a different idea. He was pleasant enough, but I sensed a danger... no, not danger, an intensity. It was off-putting."

She braced herself mentally before continuing. "I told you I had two sisters. My second oldest sister was having a long affair but ultimately did marry the man—two days before she died." Her breath caught in her throat. "Her name was Eva. Eva Braun." Her voice became cold and strident. "*That* is why I was safe from the Nazis." She looked away from him and stared at the coffee table.

Then...

An arm came around her shoulders. She stiffened. *No...*

"Greta... Gretl."

It had been so long since anyone had called her by her real

name. It took her a second for the name to register. She started to cry... and cry. Great wracking sobs escaped her. She had never cried so hard or for so long. He held her while all the years of guilt and anger and hurt poured from her, releasing her. This man understood... and didn't hate her for it. The opposite. He admired her for her strength and fortitude, when she thought she was weak. She held on to him till the last sobs were gone and her breathing returned to normal.

He stroked her hair.

"I think *you* are the amazing one, Trevor Marsh."

She smiled at him and he stopped. A look of warmth and incredible *love* came into his eyes.

"We are the most unusual pair," she said.

He sat down and lifted her chin to face him. He moved in slowly and gave her the most heart-breaking kiss she could ever imagine. She loved this man. After only one evening, she had feelings she didn't know she was capable of.

He withdrew his lips and said, "The *most* unusual pair." He looked at her deeply. "Do you want me to leave?"

Her heart pounded. "I want you to stay with me forever."

And he did.

3

AUDITION OF A LIFETIME

Doris Parmett

Marlie O'Brien's hopes and dreams hung in the balance.

Except for award-winning director Gus Avanti, two talent scouts—one of whom kept checking his texts messages—and several executive producers seated behind a long wooden table, the room was bare.

She waited for the director's signal to begin reading the script she'd been given. Instead, he set aside his copy of the script.

"Marlie O'Brien, suppose you tell me why you think you're right for this part? It says here..." He held up her résumé. "Mmm. Let's see. Okay, you were in the high school drama club and acted in high school plays, had the lead in two of them. You got a theater degree in college, but your only professional credential is a walk-on part in one Off-Broadway show. Wouldn't you agree this résumé isn't very impressive? At best, it's sparse."

Knowing this would come up, she had prepared herself beforehand. In a polite, professional tone, she replied, "Mr. Avanti, if this were for a different role, I might agree with you. However, I assure you I am a fast learner. For the specialized role of detecting card sharks, I am absolutely qualified."

"Really? Go on. So far I like the tone of your voice. Not squeaky. Continue."

"I have excellent eye-hand coordination. You won't need to pay a double for my close-up scenes. Some of my other skills include counting cards, dealing cards so that certain ones are placed where I need them, and spotting cheaters. Plus, I'm a math whiz. I don't say this to pat myself on the back but to assure you that if you give me the part, I won't disappoint you. Please consider me for *The Gamblers*."

Marlie took a deep breath. She only prayed the group couldn't see her knees knocking. In all her twenty-five years, she'd never been this nervous. With good reason. After reading an article in *Variety* announcing tryouts for *The Gambler*, a new cable television series to be set in Las Vegas, she had taken a gamble. On summer break from her job as a preschool teacher in New York, she had headed west to Tinseltown to make her dream a reality.

Gus set aside her résumé. "That's quite a speech, young lady. Let's see if it's a bunch of baloney. Are you familiar with Ben Mezrich's bestseller, *Bringing Down the House*?"

"Yes, It's the story of six MIT students who won millions in Vegas."

"You think you're as smart as they were? They were caught eventually."

"I'm smart enough to know the house always wins. I much prefer acting to gambling."

Gus was silent for a minute as he studied her. "I'm a very busy man these days, Ms. O'Brien. Unfortunately, the deal we had to shoot the series on site in Vegas fell through. Right now I'm under pressure to complete finding my cast, and then I have to find a new venue where we'll shoot. So I'll tell you what. Either I just heard a bunch of highfalutin' bragging, or you're the real thing. *The Gamblers* is about a team of undercover detectives that brings down the bad guys. I've decided to test you in action, in a real casino setting. Prove to me that you're not just a pretty face, but can deliver. If you know anything about the way I work, you know I pride myself on giving my audiences a realistic experience. For now, I'll take you at your word you're not a gambler. What about drugs and liquor. Any problems?"

"No, none."

"Okay. Tomorrow afternoon meet me in Las Vegas at the Excelsior Hotel. It's got the sort of classy, old-world charm I want for my new series." He turned to one of the producers. "Have you tried to get the Excelsior for the shooting?"

The woman shook her head. "I'll get my assistant on it."

Gus turned back to Marlie. "Furthermore, I expect my entire crew to ensure *The Gamblers* lives up to its hype. This includes the cast's publicity. I warn you, Ms. O'Brien, if you're spotted, if security tells you to leave, forget about the part. I have two seasoned actors vying for this role. Try not to screw it up. My assistant will give you the particulars. Good luck."

*

A day later Marlie was in Las Vegas, at the elegant Excelsior Hotel, feeling distinctly out of place wearing the dowdiest outfit she could find in a thrift store: dull brown skirt, faded brown blouse, and brown flats. To complete the "costume," she'd purchased a pair of tinted tortoiseshell eyeglasses to disguise her green eyes. The lenses weren't prescription; she had twenty-twenty vision. As a final touch, she'd pulled her thick mop of red hair back in a severe bun rather than wear it loose. Her only decoration was her special hair barrette.

The dealer finished dealing cards to the six people sitting around the Pai Gow poker table, and Marlie went to work. She stood behind her mark: an elderly man sitting with a stack of hundred dollar chips. By prearrangement, Gus sat opposite him wearing a fake Rolex watch adapted to receive her signals. To retain his seat at the table, he bet low. His primary goal was watching her audition.

For the next five minutes, the cacophony of noises in the room faded into the background as Marlie covertly sent Gus the cards the elderly man held close to his chest. Gus's every glance at his watch was casual and didn't draw the dealer's attention. She was pleased that Gus didn't act on her information. Staying in character, she recorded the next hand her quarry held and sent it to Gus. So far the audition was going off without a hitch. Last night she had let herself dream of signing a contract and becoming a featured player on a hit show. Who knew? Maybe one day she'd win an Emmy.

If she did get the part, she'd have to find a temporary job to fill in the gap between now and when rehearsals started. For the moment she was staying with a friend in Los Angeles. Once rehearsals and shooting began, she'd have to find a place to stay in Vegas.

As prearranged, Gus didn't win the next hand either. Marlie checked the time. Gus had allotted thirty minutes for this audition, more than he usually did. He'd told her since this was a lead role, he needed to make certain he chose the right actor.

Someone jostled her. Without turning around, she shrugged the person off. Whoever it was tapped her on the shoulder. "Stop," she hissed.

"Miss," a definite male voice said in her ear. "I'd appreciate it if you'd come with me."

She still didn't turn. "Not now, I'm busy."

"I insist."

She glanced across the table and saw what she dreaded most: a frowning Gus pursing his lips in disgust. He told the dealer he was out, pushed back his chair, and walked away. All this without attempting to speak to her. He didn't have to. She already knew she'd blown the audition—thanks to the man standing so close to her she could feel his breath.

"Miss," the intruder repeated.

Marlie swiveled around. She bumped into a solid male chest. A pair of hands clamped around her arms, steadying her. Furious, she noted quickly the broad-shouldered, dark-haired man towered over her. She judged him to be a good six foot three. Compared to her five feet four inches, he was a giant. She stared into a pair of silvery gray eyes that perused her face with no apology.

"Couldn't you see I was busy?" she snapped.

"Frankly, no. I only saw your back. Come with me. We need to talk."

"I'm not in the habit of talking to strangers. Besides, I'm in a hurry. Let me pass. I need to meet someone."

"If you mean the man who was seated across the table from you, he's gone."

Her stomach took a nosedive. This stranger had ruined everything. If not for him, she could have landed the part. Instead, whoever this man was, he had not only destroyed her chance of getting the part, he seemed to know she had been communicating with Gus. So much for proving she couldn't get caught.

"Don't make this harder on yourself," he said.

Rather than create a fuss, she let him guide her past a group of happy senior citizens seated at a row of one-armed bandits. Marlie found herself in a carpeted hallway across from a bank of elevators. She yanked her hand from his.

"Mister, I don't know you. You've already ruined my life, so now go away. If you don't, I'll call the head of security and have you thrown in jail for assault."

His response to her stern threat was to roll his eyes, reach into his suit jacket pocket, and thrust a business card into her hand. Printed in bold black letters the card read: Victor Harrison, Head of Security. She gulped. Talk about lousy luck.

"You? You're the head of security?"

His lips quirked. "'Fraid so. Also general manager and part owner of the Excelsior. I have to hand it to you. You're good, but I'm better. If your partner had acted on your signals, you'd both be in hot water."

Involving Gus would guarantee her permanent undoing. She didn't dare bring him into this. "I don't know what you're talking about."

Her interrogator raised an eyebrow. "Sure you do. Come upstairs to my office. We'll sit down and have a nice chat. Get to know each other. Then you'll tell me what I want to know."

Time to test her acting skills. Better be an Academy-Award-winning performance. "I will not. I never go anywhere with strangers. You could be lying through your teeth. That business card you handed me could be a fake, a ploy you use to trap women into going who knows where with you. For all I know, you're not only a liar, you could be a thief. Or worse, a rapist. Or maybe you hit the trifecta and are all three."

He shook his head. "You about through?" He took out a cell phone, called someone named Luke. He told him to meet him by the elevators on the west side.

In less than a minute, a huge, muscular man who could pass for a prize-winning wrestler joined them. On his jacket he wore a badge that read Security. "Yes, boss?"

"Luke, please tell this lady who I am. She's got quite a vivid imagination."

41

"You're Victor Harrison."

"Please tell her what I do here."

Luke raised his bushy eyebrows. "Miss, Mr. Harrison runs the place. He's also one of the owners."

"Now tell her how we know each other."

Luke stared at him for a few seconds. "For several years I served proudly under Colonel Harrison. He's a highly decorated Marine. If I were you, I'd do exactly what he says. Don't pick a fight with him. You'll lose. Compared to him, you're a pipsqueak, if you don't mind my saying so."

Vic coughed. "That's more than enough, Luke. Thanks."

Dismayed, Marlie stared up at Vic as Luke ambled away. "I sincerely hope you don't give me any more grief," Vic said. "Now be nice and come with me to my office."

Desperate to find Gus and make things right, Marlie played her last card. "Not so fast, buster. The world is filled with fakes. Men who lure women into their traps. After they get what they want, they murder them. What proof do I have you two characters aren't in cahoots? You've done enough damage. I don't know if I'll be able to salvage my appointment. So if you won't let me pass until we have this talk you insist on having, we'll have it right here." She tapped the face of her watch. "You have exactly two minutes before I start screaming."

Vic rolled his eyes heavenward. "In that case, I'll just remove your glasses."

"What for?"

"So I can see the screamer clearly. And do me a favor, take off your barrette."

Before Marlie could protest, her glasses were in his hand. She had the beginnings of a real headache. Reaching up, she removed the plastic barrette she'd worn as part of her costume, opened her purse, and dropped it in. Then she wiggled her fingers for him to return her glasses. Satisfied her belongings were safely in her bag, she shook her hair loose and massaged her scalp. He watched her the whole time.

"Am I amusing you?" she asked.

"On the contrary, I'm a bit awestruck. An emerald-eyed redhead. Is that your natural color?"

"My eyes or my hair?"

He raised an eyebrow. "What do you think?"

She tilted her head far back enough to see the flare of genuine interest in his silver gaze. "Of course it's real. Red hair runs in my family. Both my parents have red hair. Are you about through? Because now that you've made a mess of everything, I need to catch a bus back to Los Angeles and see if I can untangle it. I can't waste time. Unlike you, I need a job. And you've used up your two minutes."

"Hold it! You're getting ahead of me. Look, I'm who I said I am. You haven't been trespassed. If that were the case, I would have had Luke do the honors. Before you tore off on a tangent, I was going to tell you about our new advertising promotion. It's not a major program, but one to make our daytime visitors happy. A bell rang in my office letting me know you're the five-hundredth person who entered the main gambling room today. I spotted you from the window in my office and came down to tell you you'd won a small prize. This is good publicity for all parties concerned. Unless, of course, you're already wanted by the police?"

"You're actually serious. What's the prize?"

He chuckled. "Dinner with the manager. Or lunch."

She wanted to punch herself in the head, after she punched him. "Fire whoever dreamed up this stupid idea." When she saw the laughter in his eyes, she yelped, "You? You're the idiot responsible?" He nodded.

"When I approached you," he said, "I realized you were transmitting the cards from the man sitting in front of you to the man seated opposite him. Most people wouldn't catch on, but I'm not most people. Like I said, I'm better than you are. For a beautiful woman, you've chosen the wrong line of work."

Two things registered. One: this man, who ranked as probably the most handsome man she'd ever seen, a man comfortable in his own skin, a man who could easily pass for a movie star, had called her beautiful. Two: he knew she knew her way around cards. If she chose, she could be a good card cheat. Maybe not as good at cards as he claimed to be, but good enough to have landed the role of her dreams.

Cut your losses, she told herself. Leave, hightail it back to Los Angeles, get a job. If by some miracle Gus was willing to talk to her again, she could leave out the first part of Vic catching her and skip to the second, convincing Gus Vic had spoken to her because of this

43

ludicrous prize. She then might be able to salvage her audition and still be considered for the part in *The Gamblers*. A big maybe.

"What's your name?" Vic asked.

"My name is Marlie O'Brien. FYI, I'm not a cheat," she declared with righteous indignation. "Furthermore, I've never been in trouble with the law. I've never even been cited for a traffic violation or a parking ticket. Those are facts. What you saw before was my partner not acting on any of my signals."

He shoved his hands in his pockets. "Good. We're finally getting somewhere. At least now you're admitting to sending information. Which makes me wonder whether this was a dry run. Was it?"

Damn, she was off to a bad start. "All right. I just said I did read the old gentleman's cards. I admit I sent the hand he was holding to the man you mentioned, but we didn't profit from it. We never intended to profit from it. Please, you have to believe me. What you saw wasn't a dry run. I have valid reasons for my actions. Before I explain everything, there's something I must do first."

"Which is?"

"I've already told you too much. Now, I'm going to find out if you're really who you say you are. If you told me the unvarnished truth, we'll sit and talk. Otherwise, forget it."

His face grew hard. "Correction. You'll talk."

"Oh, for goodness sake. Let's not quibble over semantics."

"Marlie, has anyone ever told you you're adorable, but you're still a pain? All right, go ahead, but I'm coming with you."

He stood next to her as she waylaid two casino guards and asked if they knew the man at her side.

The guards looked at Vic. Vic shrugged. "Go ahead. You might as well tell her. The lady has trust issues."

They did. Their answers were succinct and full of praise for their boss. "Time's up," Vic said. The next thing she knew, he had escorted her into an elevator.

*

Marlie stepped into Vic's office. She took a moment to absorb its furnishings, and then crossed the room to the large windows along one wall.

"I see where these windows let you watch the action on the

casino floor. I suppose it's essential for you to check on the gamblers and your staff. Your office suits you. Large, but not frilly or pretentious. You probably hold staff meetings at that conference table. This decor is definitely masculine, not glittery or over the top. It's a very nice office. Functional, don't you agree?"

Marlie knew she was babbling inanely. Dealing with Vic felt like playing a cat and mouse game. She preferred to be the cat. The way he was watching her, she was beginning to feel like the mouse.

He strode over to the bar. "Marlie, sit down on the sofa. Now, if you're through rating my office, mind telling me your preference?"

"My preference is to leave."

"Besides that. I'll give you a choice. Soda or water?"

"Coffee. Black."

He held up two K-Cups. "Decaf or regular?"

"Water."

He switched off the Keurig, put away the cups, and reached behind the counter for a small bottle of Perrier. Handing it to her, he took a seat beside her. "Start talking. I'll know if you're lying. Is your name really Marlie O'Brien?"

"Yes."

"What did you and your partner hope to gain?"

"Me. I hoped to get a role in his new television series. You blew my chance."

"How?"

"Gus Avanti—the man sitting across the table—is the director of a new cable series. He challenged me to see if I lived up to my claims in an actual casino setting. He selected the Excelsior. Gus appreciates authenticity. He prefers shooting on location rather than in a studio. Unfortunately, a deal he thought he had secured with another hotel fell through."

"What sort of deal?"

"Where he'll film *The Gamblers.* His people are trying to find a new location, preferably in a casino here in Vegas."

"How do you know this?"

"He told me. And he talked with one of the producers about it. I don't care where we film so long as I get the part. Two other actors are competing for the same role."

Vic seemed to absorb what she was saying. "Why you? What's your acting experience? When you're not trying out for an acting job,

45

how do you earn a living?"

Marlie blew out a breath. "I teach preschool at a private school in New York. We're on summer break. Acting's always been my first love, but it's a tough business. Besides talent, an actor needs a lucky break. Timing is vital. Helps to know someone. And I'd never try out on a director's couch."

His attention zeroed in on her face. "Has anyone asked you to?"

"Yes, and I refused."

"Good for you. All right, what's your experience?"

"Aside from lead roles in high school and a degree in theater from a top college, plus one Off-Broadway walk-on, not much. I still have to pay the bills. This was my dream opportunity. You killed it," she said bitterly.

"How does gambling come into this?"

"When I first met with the talent scout, I went for broke. I told him I could spot a card cheater, could count cards, the works. He recommended me for an audition. Gus, the director, wanted proof in a real casino setting that I just wasn't handing him a line. He said that because of my light acting experience, this was the only way he'd consider me for the role. Then you barged into my life." Tears welled up in her eyes and spilled over. Marlie dug into her purse for a tissue.

"I read up on Vegas to impress him," she went on. "El Rancho Vegas opened in 1941 but burned down in 1960. That's the same year Louis 'The Lip' LaFica built the Excelsior, isn't it?"

"Yes. Vegas has changed quite a bit since then. Most hotels on the strip are mega-establishments. We cater to families. Plus, we keep up with modernization. I'm pleased to say the Excelsior has retained its exclusivity."

"My parents eloped to Vegas. They were married in the Graceland Chapel. Mom adored Elvis and wanted a signature Elvis wedding in Las Vegas. She's saved the silk flowers and other memorabilia from the ceremony. Vic, do you believe me?"

"Give me the barrette you stashed in your purse."

Her stomach took yet another nosedive. "Why do you want my barrette?"

He waved his hand. "To remove the hidden camera you've configured in that decorative swan attached to the top. Marlie, I told you I'm better at this game than you. Now hand it over."

She slapped it into his hand. "There! Satisfied?"

46

"Call it your swan song. Now, if you've told me the truth, I need to know who taught you."

She jutted out her jaw. "My father, and don't you dare say one bad thing about him. We did it for fun. From the time I learned to count, my father found a way to keep me from being bored. I can't help being a math whiz."

Vic stared at her in amazement. "How old were you at the time?"

Sitting primly, she folded her hands. "Seven. The teacher was very impressed."

"I bet."

Marlie chuckled. "She was."

"It's a wonder she didn't arrange a parent/teacher conference."

Keeping a straight face, Marlie said, "She did, trust me."

"What happened?"

"My dad kissed her."

Vic's brows rose. "He did what?"

"Kissed her. On the lips."

"Did she have him arrested for sexual harassment?"

Marlie laughed. "Hardly. She kissed him back. Mom was my teacher. She homeschooled me until the fourth grade. My parents made me promise never to show the principal of my new school my skills or teach another student my tricks."

Vic roared with laughter. "Who came up with the idea of configuring the camera on the barrette and that fake Rolex to receive the pictures you were sending?"

The question caught her off guard. Biting her lip to keep a straight face, Marlie said, "When my dad learned I was coming to Vegas to audition, he kind of suggested a way to beat the odds. Thanks to you, it didn't work. How do you know so much?"

Struggling to control his laughter, Vic replied, "Luke didn't add I commanded an intelligence unit. I admit, your dad's clever, but he should have told you to wear a ring with a hidden camera. The swan was a dead giveaway. Incidentally, what line of work is your father in?"

"You're sure you want to know?"

"Positive."

"Dad's a professional hacker for the government."

Vic whistled. "Does your mother still teach?"

"No. Mom retired last summer. My dad is thinking of retiring. If I had gotten the part in *The Gamblers*, they planned on moving here. We're a tight family."

"Brothers and sisters?"

"Just me. Vic, I'd say it's been pleasant, but it hasn't. I'd like to leave now."

Rather than walk her to the door, he waved her over to his desk as he took a seat behind it. "How often do you gamble? For real? The truth, please."

"I don't. I don't have the stomach for it. Money is too hard to come by."

"Spoken like a preschool teacher. That's your problem."

Indignant, she said, "You're my problem. I was doing just fine until you spoiled everything."

"Marlie, a professional is a gambler who can shed one persona and adopt another. Can you do that?"

"That's exactly what I was doing until you came along. I don't usually dress like this." She turned to leave. "If you're through with me, I'm going."

In a fast move, he stepped away from his desk. His arm shot out and drew her back. "You've made your point. It's true what they say about pissing off a redhead. Since you think I ruined your chances at your dream role, let me make it up to you. I feel responsible for ruining your audition."

She folded her arms across her chest. "Exactly how do you intend to make it up to me?"

"Mmm, give me a second. All right. For starters, you said you need a job. I can help you in that department."

"How? Waiting tables? I warn you, I could have a case of the dropsies."

"Marlie, calm down. I'm trying to make things right."

She scoffed. "Unless you're a director offering me a juicy part in a surefire, about-to-be-a-hit series or a movie, you can't make this right. I had a chance. A one in a million chance. You blew it for me."

"Marlie," he said flatly. "I didn't command a Marine unit without skills. In civilian lingo, we go by the time-honored slogan: If at first you don't succeed, try, try again."

When she only scowled at him, he continued, "Job first. I'll pay you to be a card spotter. As good as our security people are, we can always use another person on our team."

"If I agree, it's temporary. I'm still going to try to patch things up with Gus. If that doesn't work, then I'll keep auditioning whenever I can. However, I'm also due back in school in September."

"Fair enough. As an Excelsior employee, the job—even temporary ones—comes with benefits: health, discounts in our stores, meals during working hours."

She clutched at the morsel of hope. "How much?"

Smiling, he named a very generous amount.

Marlie did a quick calculation. "When do I start?"

"Tomorrow."

She shook her head. "Impossible. I need to go back to Los Angeles, where I've been staying at a friend's. All of my clothes are there. I wore this outfit to show Gus I could fade into the background."

Vic's gaze flew to her face, then he slowly let his eyes roam from the top of her head downward. "Marlie, you know what I see when I see you?"

Feeling as though he had just undressed her with his eyes, she ignored the fluttering in her stomach and answered, "I think I'm afraid to ask."

He fell silent for a few seconds and then said, "I see a stubborn, feisty, intelligent, titian-haired beauty. A woman, who for reasons I can't explain to myself, has thoroughly captivated me. I see a determined young woman who flew across the country to make her dreams a reality. I see a strong-minded woman with an unwavering desire to succeed as an actress, although she is already succeeding as a teacher. Because I've been instrumental in dashing her dreams, I'm determined to right the wrong I inflicted."

Stunned and utterly surprised, Marlie swallowed. "Is that what you really see?"

Reverting to business, he nodded. Then he took a checkbook from his desk drawer and quickly filled in a check. "Please, this isn't a gift. Use it to buy a spectacular outfit for our luncheon appointment with Gus."

"W-what luncheon appointment?" she stuttered, thoroughly flabbergasted.

"What's Gus Avanti's phone number?" She fumbled for her cell phone, found the number, and gave it to him. He dialed, switched his desk phone to speaker, and said, "Listen and learn."

She could hear the phone ring on the other end, and then a man answered. "Hello, who is this?"

Marlie heard Gus's voice.

"Glad I caught you," Vic said. "My name is Victor Harrison. I run the Excelsior Hotel here in Vegas. I noticed you at one of our tables earlier. I'm sorry you left so abruptly, but I can appreciate how busy you are hiring a cast for your new production. I won't take up too much of your time. I'm here in my office with Marlie O'Brien, the actress you were auditioning. I'm sorry I interrupted her audition. She's a whiz with cards, as I'm sure you know. We've been testing each other's skills.

"I wanted to explain to you that I came downstairs earlier to tell her she'd won a prize. The hotel's launching a new advertising program. The Excelsior constantly launches new advertising programs. Anything to promote business. While the Excelsior comps repeat and high-rolling players, we felt we should focus on the more casual gambler, the daytime visitor who comes to Vegas for pure fun. As our initial winner, Marlie will get her fair share of publicity. I'm sure you appreciate free publicity. Anyway, that's not the reason I called. I understand you're looking for a place to film *The Gamblers*. Why don't we meet for lunch tomorrow and talk about you using the Excelsior?"

At first, Marlie couldn't believe Vic's gall. Then as he kept talking, her mouth dropped open. This guy was one smooth operator. Before the call ended, Gus had agreed to meet with him to discuss details.

"Please tell Marlie I said hello," Gus added.

Smiling, Vic set the phone on the receiver. "That's taken care of. You're in the clear. You now have a clean start. I come along with it, of course."

"You do?"

"I do. But first, I need to know more about you."

"I told you everything," she said.

"Not the most important stuff. To begin with, are you married? Not all women wear a wedding ring when trying to impress a director."

"No."

"Engaged?"

"No."

"Significant other?"

"Not at the present time. Are you married?"

"No."

"Engaged?"

"No."

"Significant other?"

He rose. Giving her a dazzling smile, he replied, "I have a feeling I'm about to have one very soon. Marlie, this is new territory for me. Normally, my staff takes over when there's a problem on the casino floor. But when I saw you, for reasons that boggle my mind, in your case, I couldn't do that. I think there's something special between us. Shall we take a gamble, see where it goes?"

She was already halfway there. Here was a knight in shining armor who kept his word. He made things more than better. He opened up the world for her. "I only bet on a sure thing," she said.

"So do I. We'll sign a contract and make this official."

"A standard contract?" she asked, returning his smile.

"Not a standard contract. A special contract. A one-of-a-kind contract."

Without waiting for permission, he gathered her in his arms and lowered his head. What started out as a friendly peck on the cheek soon turned into a tender meeting of lips. Marlie was shocked—and thrilled—when the tender kiss quickly became one of raw passion.

On both sides.

Later, when both came down to earth, they agreed it was a very special one-of-a-kind contract.

4

ILLUSIONS

Jennifer St. Giles

Therefore trust to thy heart,
And to what the world calls illusions.
Henry Wadsworth Longfellow

Prologue
New Year's Day 1972
Manhattan, New York

The luxurious comforts of the Plaza did little to ease the sense of impotence gripping Assistant Deputy Director Tollie Clydsen's gut. Everything gained over the decades—the power and the fear—was slipping like fine sand from the Director's iron fist. Age was the one enemy that neither he, nor the formidable man at his side could defeat. Jay Allen Cooper, his friend, his mentor, his world, had built the FBI into a tool that had made and broken presidents, as well as shaped the nation, and the world.

"When I'm gone, Tollie, the vultures will come and rip my legacy apart. And if Nick Richards is still in office, he'll oust you. Your years of devotion will mean nothing."

Tollie elbowed his longtime friend. Neither of them wanted to admit death marched near, but they had to face it. Their reign over the FBI was almost over. "The bastard will be doing me a favor. I'll have little heart for the job without your genius driving the game. But you worry for nothing. Our time hasn't come yet."

Jay smiled and clapped Tollie on the shoulder. "You're right. We've time. Sometimes the cold in my bones brings a cloud of doubt over me."

"Then we should be celebrating your birthday in Miami and not New York."

"And break with tradition? *Never*. I heard from Mark. Surveillance reveals Richards may hang himself. All we have to do is sit back and watch."

Tollie shook his head. "Hang himself? Literally or figuratively?"

"Does it matter?"

"Have you arranged—"

"For a quick resolution? No. A slow political death is what this director orders for him."

Tollie laughed.

"Which brings me back to the vultures. I've left enough information in my not-so-secret files to satisfy their thirst for blood. The rest will go to the grave with us."

"Will it? What about the loose ends with the Kincaids?" Jay had proven the best way to kill an enemy's power was to eliminate his sons.

"There are safeguards in place. She's being watched and he knows both her and his son will die if he talks. The secret is safe in the illusions of the past."

Illusions were everything. They were the master tool in gaining power and control of the masses. They could destroy any man, create any icon, hide any truth, and obscure any crime. The man at his side had used them well.

HEADLINE NEWS:
May 2, 1972 FBI Director Jay Allen Cooper found dead of a heart attack in his Washington home. Assistant Director Tollie Clydsen to serve as interim Director.

May 3, 1972 President Nick Richards appoints Mark Gray to replace Tollie Clydsen as Director of the FBI.

June 1972

Last night I dreamed of Excelsior, of my father falling from its granite and glass tower, of him screaming with no one to hear his cries for help. I'd awakened with my heart racing and the vicious wrath of a thunderstorm pounding my home.

The sense of doom that had always hovered over me like a ghostly mist mushroomed into a dark cloud. Death seemed but a breath away. Shivering beneath the covers, despite the summer temperatures, I closed my eyes and tried to pretend the life of Hannity Valentine, my life, wasn't just an illusion.

But it was.

Yesterday morning, on my twenty-first birthday, I learned the details of my inheritance from my father's attorneys, Mr. Giovanni and Mr. Luca—Chicago natives from suits to wingtips. I couldn't believe what they had said.

"I'm sorry, Mr. Giovanni. Can you repeat that please?"

"Your father died deeply in debt. You inherited Meryl La Roe's house from her, but the rest of her estate, when it's finally settled, will go to charity for the mentally ill."

"Then how have I lived all these years? The staff? My schooling? My clothes? My bank account? How has all this been possible?"

Mr. Giovanni cleared his throat. "I'm not at liberty to say who your benefactor is. But after your father's death, he arranged for everything. He hired Meryl's staff to take care of you, and each year he has provided a generous sum for your well-being. Now that you're old enough and have requested to handle your own finances, he is willing to continue that support under one condition."

"And what would that be?"

"You're never to seek his identity. All funds will be sent to us and we'll issue payment to you." He pushed a contract and pen my way. "Just sign right here."

I stared at the small print before me until my vision blurred, feeling as if gilded prison bars I'd lived behind were about to destroy my first bid for freedom.

Growing up the only child of the *Great Valentino*, my life had been filled with strangers as my family traveled from city to city doing magic shows. My mother had been his assistant, and I had been, according to him, his inspiration and best critic. At least three or four times a year, whenever Meryl could do so between films or appearances, she'd come to see us. Meryl and my mother had grown up in foster care together, and even though Meryl had become a famous actress, she stayed close to my mother. They were happy years. Then, when I was nine, my mother became ill and died. Meryl had been the one who'd cried with me and had held me until I could breathe again. Gina, her assistant, Sophie, her housekeeper, and Tony, her driver, had taken care of us all, until my father and I moved to Las Vegas and he became a teacher at the Magical Arts Institution directed by Arthur Van Rathum, the famous "Phantom Magician." I discovered a new mother in Arthur's wife, Jenna Vive, and the painful throes of puppy love in their fifteen-year-old son, Lance. Two years later, my world ended in a harrowing chain of events.

First, my father and I abruptly departed from Las Vegas after a storm of angry arguments between Arthur Van Rathum and my father. My father refused to explain why. We went to Meryl and stayed with her at her new house in Los Angeles for a time. She'd shared all of her grand plans to renovate with us, but I could tell something was wrong. I learned what that was the night before we left. They thought I was sleeping, but I'd wakened and heard them talking. Meryl told my father she had evidence that powerful people planned to kill a man she cared greatly about, and that she feared for her own life too.

We returned the next day to Las Vegas in a hurry, where my father planned to see Arthur Van Rathum. We awoke the next morning to the news that Meryl had died in her new home. My father died at the Excelsior Hotel that night.

I was eleven years old.

Since then, doctors and psychiatrists had tried to convince me to accept the truth. That Meryl and my father had chosen to leave me and committed suicide. She, through a drug overdose, and he, by leaping from Excelsior's balcony. I refused to believe it then and I didn't believe it now. The doctors labeled me as troubled and delicate, delusional over the past and paranoid about the future. They prescribed medications that I rarely took because I didn't want to lose my memories and perceptions of the past. They had been killed. I had no doubt of it, and I always felt it could happen to me too.

Learning I had a benefactor changed everything for me. Whoever it was, had to know something about why Meryl and my father had been killed. Why else had they provided so lavishly for me for ten years?

Mr. Giovanni cleared his throat. "Are you feeling all right, Miss Valentine?"

I snapped my gaze to his. It was always there, the innuendo that I wasn't quite one hundred percent. "I'm perfectly fine. I'm thinking over the condition."

"Are you mad?" Mr. Luca interjected, genuinely shocked. "It would be insane to turn down the offer of a life of ease."

Mr. Giovanni pointed out some disturbing realities. "I must inform you that if you don't sign, all future payments end today. You'll no longer be able to afford the lifestyle to which you've been accustomed. Only your education will be paid for from this point on. You can keep what funds are currently in your account, but I can tell you they won't cover the expense of the staff you employ or the leased car for even a month more. You can avoid all of that trouble. All you have to do is sign."

How could I sign? After ten years of lingering doubts, unanswered questions, and plaguing nightmares, I finally had a lead, and the impetus to hunt for the truth. I had chosen to study investigative journalism for a reason. It was time.

A disturbance from an irate client in the reception interrupted our conversation and had both Mr. Giovanni and Mr. Luca leaping to their feet and rushing to the door. I heard the yelling coming from the other room, but didn't pay attention to what the man was upset about. I had one purpose in mind, to peek inside my file on Mr. Giovanni's desk. I quickly stood and flipped the file open. I'd been told often from my father and Meryl that I had an impeccable memory, and the older I grew, the more I realized how true that was. Especially now.

As soon as I saw Excelsior Enterprises was the source of my sustenance, I knew there could only be one man funding my life. I left the attorneys sputtering as I declined my benefactor's offer.

I spent a troubled night dreaming about my father, his death at the Excelsior, and the Van Rathums. My heart raced with both fear and anticipation when I made the decision to confront Arthur Van Rathum today. *The Phantom Magician* was one of the longest running shows in Las Vegas. I knew exactly where to find him.

In the wake of the TWA bomb situation in March, one of which had exploded in Las Vegas, I wasn't about to fly. After arguing rather strongly with Gina and Tony about the safety of my planned venture today, I packed a bag and drove for Las Vegas. Their concerns had been valid. I'd just recently received my driver's license and had I never traveled alone before. But I had to escape my gilded cage and this was the first step.

Storms followed me from Los Angeles, roiling ominously over the desert and mountains with dark clouds and bolts of lightning. My memories of the Van Rathums seemed just as tumultuous—especially of Lance. He'd been a blue-eyed devil who'd captured my imagination in inexplicable ways and always managed to make my heart pound. Usually in fear. Though his father had insisted on Lance learning all there was to know about the magic trade, Lance's passion had been motorcycles. His stunts had turned my stomach. Spurred on by his Belgian relatives, all Lance ever spoke of was beating Rene Beaten, the Motor Cross World Champion.

He'd filled my young heart with wonder, once by magically producing a bouquet of flowers in an elaborate trick using his father's unlockable magic box. In my mind, I still heard Lance's teasing words, "Flowers for a forever Valentine." He was being witty with my name and I knew it, but I cherished the flowers. Even had the dried petals preserved in wax paper and pressed in the pages of my diary.

But all of that had changed in a heartbeat, then disappeared.

Driving up to the Excelsior Hotel, I shoved my memories aside and exited the shiny, gold Cadillac Coupe De Ville. The coming storm felt as if it had raised the temperature rather than lowered it. Firmly handing the valet my key, I accepted the receipt, amazed how subtle things bolstered my budding independence. Drawing a deep breath, I shouldered my purse and clutched my overnight bag. Made of hard leather and heavy gold, the bag felt like an armored shield as I faced the Excelsior's brooding façade. Still, I shivered despite the desert heat beating down on me.

My father died here. I didn't plan to die here, but neither had he. Secrets killed.

"Good afternoon and welcome to the Excelsior. May I carry your bag?" Shifting my gaze, I met the offer of help with a determined smile. I would find the truth. The bellman was clean-cut, and wore a crisp uniform with his friendliness.

"No, thank you." I held onto my bag. I'd just navigated my first solo trip from home and wanted to keep every shred of independence.

"If you're sure. The registration desk is inside on the left."

"I'm sure." He turned to assist two gentlemen in black suits exiting from a black and silver car.

Resolve bolstered, I headed for the revolving doors. The moment I stepped forward, with the glass doors moving to trap me, one of the black-suited men rudely rushed into the space with me.

I'd recently seen *The Godfather* and immediately felt uncomfortable as I recalled Don Cuneo had been assassinated in a revolving door. The man was tall with dark hair and tinted sunglasses.

"My apologies, miss," he said. "I didn't see you."

For some reason, I didn't believe him. I hugged the door in front of me, moving forward so quickly that I exited into the lobby off-balanced. I scrambled to stay upright.

A genius of an architect had placed a black marble fountain in the center of the circular area just over a dozen or so feet from the entrance, an impressive sight to immediately see. And had I not tripped over several bags sitting on the floor next to an elderly woman wearing pink flamingo sunglasses, I would have been fine. Now I wasn't.

Excelsior meant the highest peak of excellence—in other words, on top of the world. In the fountain, a statue of a naked, perfectly sculpted man stood upon a globe, and I was about to nose-dive into the dregs of that world at my worst.

"Hold on there." Laughing, a nearby man grabbed my arm and took hold of my overnight bag as he jerked me to a stop before disaster. "Fountains are better after midnight," he said, softly. His deep tone rumbled intimately between us.

"Thank you for saving me," I gasped. He was tall and I had to angle my neck to meet his gaze, his very blue and somewhat familiar gaze.

His grin was as sensual as the twinkle in his eyes. "Don't thank me yet. I might tempt you into skinny-dipping at midnight."

"Lance Van Rathum?" I asked in disbelief.

His brows drew to a point. "Who are—Hannity Valentine?"

"Yes," I said, relieved and surprised. Ten years ago, he'd gone into the army. I hadn't expected to actually see him, but in the back of my mind I had hoped to hear about him. "This is unbelievable. I've come to see your father."

His warm gaze turned arctic. "I'm sorry you've wasted your time. That isn't possible." He turned on his heel and walked away.

I blinked, taken aback as the sting of the past needled my heart. His parting words years ago had been, *I'm sorry I ever met your father or you.*

I marched after him. "Hold on! You can't do that!" This time I grabbed his arm and yanked him to a stop. Or more accurately, he let me stop him. I imagine as broad-chested and firmly muscled as he was, there would be little I could do to keep him from doing anything he wanted.

"Go back to Los Angeles, Valentine. There is nothing here for you."

I snatched my overnight bag from him. "I don't know what happened between your father and mine years ago, but I'm not going anywhere until I see your father and get some answers. How did you know I live in Los Angeles?" I narrowed my gaze, searching his expression.

He ignored the question, looking as impenetrable as a stone wall. "Hearing from you will only upset my father. He had nothing to do with your father's suicide. Go back home and live a good life."

"My father didn't take his own life. He was mur—"

I didn't finish my sentence because Lance leaned down and planted his mouth on mine. Total, complete shock exploded inside me, but it wasn't the uppermost emotion. I didn't dare put a name to the wildfire burning through me.

He backed a breath away, his expression one of mirrored surprise. Though not pleasantly so. "I'm sorry. Don't say another word about that," he whispered. "Not here."

Blinking, I realized we'd attracted an audience. Those near us in the bustling lobby had their gazes fixed on me and him. Even the black-suited man who'd followed me into the revolving door had removed his tinted glasses and stared intently our way, far too interested for a complete stranger. For some reason, he didn't appear at all happy.

Lance glanced at his watch. "*Damn.* You'll have to come with me," he said. "I'm late to a meeting that I can't miss. We'll continue this discussion on the way... privately." Taking my elbow, he urged me across the lobby and out a side door. I juggled my overnight bag as I tried to keep pace. This was a different entrance than the one with the revolving door. He looked at his watch again. "My driver should be here by now."

While I wanted answers, I wasn't quite sure this was the smartest way to get them. "Where are you going?"

Wind from the approaching storms whipped at my plaid mini-skirt and I backed closer to the hotel, reflecting that I should have worn bell-bottoms. But vanity had won out over practicality when I'd dressed this morning. I always felt cool in my white go-go boots and matching belt.

"I've a meeting at the Sands with the contractor building my home."

My mind raced. "How do I know you're not whisking me a way to permanently put an end to my questions? You could make me disappear and—"

He laughed warmly. "You always had a wild imagination, Hani. If I remember correctly, you were very adept at spinning scenarios on how my motorcycle and I would meet an untimely end. You had my mother wringing her hands every time I rode."

I had to smile at the memory, and his use of the nickname he'd given me back then. "Did you ever beat Rene Beaten?"

His eyes widened with surprise. "You remember? Wow." He shook his head. "No, I never made it over to the European racing circuits. I found something better to do. 101st Airborne."

"I remember you left for the Army."

"My career lasted about a year, until my parachute decided to malfunction."

"Good Lord!" My free hand clasped my heart as I searched his gaze. "What happened?"

He slid his finger along the back of my hand. I swear, I felt the touch all the way to my breast. I sucked in air. "You used to do that when you were little." He dropped his hand and was all business again. "My buddy latched onto me and didn't let go. We had a rough landing, but we survived. My career ended before it ever really got off

61

the ground."

I almost jabbed him in the stomach, like I used to do, for the morbid joke. Instead, I caught my breath, realizing how close to death he had come. A man exited the hotel and stood next to us. He too wore a black suit in the Vegas heat. I found myself wishing for a tourist in a Hawaiian shirt or even a psychedelic jumpsuit.

Lance gave the guy a glance then frowned at his watch. He pointed to the line of Yellow, Checker, and Star taxi cabs lined up at the curb. "Come on. I don't know where my driver is, but I have to go. You'll feel safer in a cab anyway, right?"

"Yes," I said, my heart still racing from his touch. I wasn't fool enough to believe the cab made me *that* much safer. If Lance was of the mind to do me harm, there were any number of ways. Like put my guard at ease and strike later? I had to shake my head in self-disgust. While I was doing my best to be wise, I knew more than my guard had crumbled during our short encounter. I remembered the young man from my childhood and found it hard to truly fear him. Perhaps that familiarity was more dangerous than anything else.

We got into the first cab at the corner and Lance requested the driver go to the Sands Hotel.

He sat back as the driver sped away. Roberta Flack's newest, *The First Time Ever I Saw Your Face*, played on the radio. It wasn't a song I wanted to hear at the moment. That my sun and my moon used to rise in his eyes, as only it could in young puppy love, wasn't something I wanted to remember—but I did anyway. His charisma demanded it.

He'd already made the earth move moments ago and he hadn't even really kissed me. He had just pretended to. My experience with men was extremely limited. A few dates, a few kisses, but that was it. No one had moved me enough for me to leave my comfort zone.

Until now.

Lance's chiseled features, the same yet so vastly different than they'd been ten years ago, had already carved a place in my mind. His full, sensual lips, decidedly Roman nose, strong chin, and expressive brow left little doubt that he could be deeply passionate and infuriatingly stubborn.

"You want to tell me what in the blazes is going on, Hannity?"

"I did tell you. I came here to see your father. I want to ask him what he knows about the death of Meryl La Roe and my father."

"*Meryl La Roe?* As in the famous actress who overdosed on barbiturates?"

Squeezing my eyes shut, I prayed for strength. "Yes, that Meryl. She was my godmother and she didn't commit suicide. Neither did my father."

"What about the men in suits following you? The one in the revolving door. Then another just now."

I winced to hear him put into words what I'd begun to fear. "I've never seen them before now. Two men in a black Impala drove up to the Excelsior just after I arrived. Are they following me? Or is it just an odd coincidence? All I know is ten years ago two people I loved were murdered. Nobody wanted to hear an eleven-year-old's opinion. They patted my hand and sent me to psychiatrists. I didn't have any facts to go on and nobody to appeal to, so I had to let it go. Yesterday I turned twenty-one and met with my father's attorneys about my inheritance. Much to my surprise, I learned there was none, and never had been any. Someone else has been providing nicely for me and would continue to do so for the rest of my life. All I had to do was sign papers agreeing to never seek out my benefactor. I didn't sign, but I did manage to sneak into my file. Excalibur Enterprises has been funding my life. I remember the night my father suggested the business name to your father."

"You remember a lot for being so little."

"Vividly. Are you going to tell me I'm wrong?"

"No." He sighed. "It's a very complicated situation and there are some things you don't know. I didn't handle it all too well at the time, either. You didn't deserve my anger then."

The taxi pulled up to the entrance of the Sands Hotel. Lance handed the driver a ten dollar bill and grabbed my overnight bag. I kept hold of my purse and tried to keep my mini-skirt decent as I scooted across the seat. *Bell-bottoms would have been wiser.* Glancing up, I realized my legs had Lance's full attention, and I tingled everywhere.

At twenty-one, apart from several girlfriends who all had boyfriends, I'd had no relationships. I let the mini skirt ride an inch higher and slid my legs out.

Before I stood, his hand reached for mine in an offer of gentlemanly assistance. I took hold of his firm grip and met his gaze. He arched a knowing brow. In an instant, I knew that he knew what I'd done. The stark, honest moment of desire was there between us, and as I gained my feet, he inched slightly closer. First, my bare knee brushed against his pant leg, then my arm slid along his chest, pressing into the cloth of his suit enough to feel the hard muscle beneath.

That neither of us pulled back from the contact, shifted the dynamics between us from the realm of distant acquaintance into a world of tantalizing possibilities—one of fountains after midnight and more. And none of that had anything to do with why I had come to Las Vegas.

I'd awakened this morning having dreamed of my father's death, and burdened to find the truth. The events of the day had yet to dispel the darkening cloud over me. If anything, it had grown more real than ever. "Life has taught me that everything is complicated. If there are things I don't know, then feel free to enlighten me."

He smiled, his lips curving, until dimples graced his cheeks. "Invitation received." He set his hand to my back and eased me toward the Sands Hotel. Something was happening between us, and quickly, the desire springing easily from the roots of our past.

In my mind, I'd meant for him to tell me what I didn't know about his father, my father, and Excalibur Enterprises. But did I have another meaning behind my words as well? Did I want him to enlighten me about passion? Every singing nerve in my body stood up and shouted at the idea. I scrambled for something to say, suddenly nervous.

"We stayed here once with Meryl before my father took the job with your father," I told Lance. "It was February and my father was over the moon to be doing a show in the Copa. Not a main show, but a private one, afterward. Meryl hired my father for a surprise birthday party for one of her friends. His name was Joey Bishop. I remember that because it was posted on the marquee along with Frank Sinatra, Dean Martin, Sammy Davis Jr., and Peter Lawford. Meryl spent time with a voice instructor practicing singing *Happy Birthday* over and over. Everything had to be perfect because someone really important was staying at the hotel and was expected to secretly stop in. It must have gone well. Meryl was very happy afterwards. My father accused Meryl of being star-struck. I thought that was funny because Meryl was a star. She did the same thing again. Got all worried about singing *Happy Birthday* for President Kincaid, and you know that she met with—" Lance pressed a finger to my lips as a bellmen stepped close to open the glass entry door.

"Hannity, I'm beginning to think you're a walking time bomb. We'll talk more after my meeting. Meanwhile, try not to reveal any more memories."

"Because?"

"I don't know why. Let's just call it gut instinct for now."

A beep sounded and he pulled a pager from his pocket. "*Hell*, I forgot to call Reynolds. I was crossing the lobby to call my father's attorney when you tumbled in the door." He ushered her into the hotel and went directly to the Sandpiper Café where, according to its advertisement, family dining was at its finest.

At this time of day, the restaurant was fairly empty. Lance waved to a man at the back and we joined him. Blueprints covered one table top, coffee and a plate of sandwiches burdened another. After introductions, which regulated me to a childhood friend visiting the area, they invited me to eat while Lance and his contractor talked business. I realized that I hadn't eaten since Pop Tarts this morning.

Three cups of coffee and one and a half sandwiches later, I relaxed in my seat, my gaze automatically settling on Lance. I couldn't not look at him. He'd matured, delivered on the promise of being the devastatingly handsome man I'd seen in his younger self. But I could honestly say there was more to my attraction to him than his looks and my childhood infatuation. His excitement over the project was infectious. I could tell he'd put a lot of thought and care into making his home just right. I also noted that all aspects of the single story house were to be wheelchair accessible. Since his father was the Phantom Magician and still performing at the Excelsior's Grand Salon, I wondered if his mother was ill.

"I don't mean to pry, but who is handicapped?" I asked as soon as the contractor left with the blueprints. We were alone at the back of the restaurant.

Lance settled his gaze on me, and said something very odd. "We all have illusions of our lives, of the people in them, who they are or were. Having them dispelled takes the magic out of life. You sure you won't just return to Los Angeles and let this all go?"

"I wouldn't be close to a master's in Investigative Journalism if I could let something important go without trying to find the truth."

He shook his head, his eyes and tone suddenly sad. My chest tightened with concern. "Some truths are better off hidden in the past. My sister is in a wheelchair, and unless some miracle of medicine comes along, she may be in one permanently."

"Your sister?" I sat back shocked. I'd never seen or heard that the Van Rathums had a daughter.

He looked at me intently. "Her name is Valentine. She's nine years old. My mother named her after her father. She was injured in the car accident that killed my mother. A hit and run driver."

Shock after shock left me gasping. My hands shook and my face felt numb as my mind played back his words. "Jena Vive died?"

"Yes. Six years ago."

"You have a sister?"

"Yes."

My mother named her after her father. She's nine. Her name is Valentine.

"Are you saying that your mother and my father... that I have a sister, well, a half-sister?"

"Yes."

"And your father knew about this?"

"She told him when she found out she was pregnant. It's why our fathers argued and both of you left Las Vegas. It's why I stormed off to the Army. However hurt and angry my father was, I have to believe he didn't murder your father as you think. That wasn't who my father was. It wasn't his way. He and my mother stayed together after everything because he practiced the forgiveness he preached. Dredging this all up now and spreading rumors will only hurt Val and I can't let you do that. She has enough to deal with as it is."

I scrubbed my numb cheeks with my palms. I couldn't believe it all, but it did explain so much. "*Dear God.* This is a lot to take in. First, I am so sorry to hear about your mother. Second, I am reeling to hear I have a sister, but glad, despite the circumstances. You must know I wouldn't do anything to cause her harm. I lost my whole world close to her age now. But more importantly, I never thought your father murdered my father. Even now that you've given me cause to doubt, I don't think it. I know my father trusted yours enough to come to him for help."

Glancing to assure we were still alone, I lowered my voice. "Before Meryl La Roe died, I overheard her tell my father that she had proof that powerful people were going to kill someone important. She wanted to stop it from happening and my father told her he would help her."

"Why didn't she go to the police?" he sounded doubtful.

I closed my eyes a moment. *What would I do if Lance didn't believe me? What if he put me in the crazy box with my lawyers and the doctors?* I sucked in air, praying Lance would understand. "My father asked her that. She said the authorities were behind the planned murder. We left her, and the next day she was dead. Then my father, who would have never abandoned me, supposedly commits suicide that night?" I shook my head. "Please, you have to believe me. They were murdered and powerful people, people who were the law, were the killers. I think your father can help reveal who those powerful men were."

Lance caught my hand, leaning even closer as he whispered. "You do realize what you're implying, don't you?"

I looked him dead in the eye and whispered what I'd never allowed myself the freedom to say, though I'd wondered it many times after I'd read about my godmother's life. "Yes. President Kincaid was assassinated a little over a year after Meryl and my father's supposed suicide."

Lance closed his eyes and shook his head. "It sounds so unbelievable. Even nine years afterward."

"Does it? Have you read into the details of what happened? How convenient was it that the man suspected of the crime was assassinated just two days after the crime?"

Exhaling, he squeezed my hand tighter. "I know. I've always believed there was more to the story. So, I'm inclined to believe you may be right about this. Unfortunately, there isn't much my father can tell anyone now. Every once in a while he'll have a lucid moment, but they are rare. He has dementia, Alzheimer's to be exact. There were signs of it before the tragedy with your father, and then after my mother's death he went downhill fast."

I clung to that glimmer of belief Lance expressed. It meant more to me than I could say at that moment. "You've been through hell these past years."

Our gazes met and locked. Gone was the cocky smile and the suave seduction. The man before me now was raw and real. He knew the painful disillusions of life. "Seems as if you have been through hell too."

I frowned, suddenly puzzled. "If your father is ill, then who is the Phantom Magician then?"

"You're looking at him. I am the man who can make anything and anyone disappear through mirrors."

His pager beeped again and his brows shot up as he looked at it. "There may be someone besides my father we can talk to. Reynolds. He's been my father's attorney since I was born. He's paged me three times today. Come on." He urged me up, and paid the bill.

Purse across my shoulder, I grabbed my overnight case and followed him to the front desk. He called Reynolds. The one-sided conversation I overheard proved disturbing.

"Your warning comes too late."

"I see. Well, I've already had a very interesting conversation with Miss Valentine about the past. We'd like to see you now, if possible."

"Why? I don't want him upset."

"No. Val is at summer camp this week."

"All right. We'll meet you there." Lance hung up the phone, and without meeting my gaze, motioned for me to hurry as he walked for the exit. I was surprised I felt the lack of his touch and would have welcomed the heat of his hand upon my back again. But more than anything, I wanted to look into his eyes. Something seemed different. My old doubts hit me. Did he really believe me, or was he humoring me. "Where are we going?"

He kept walking, but answered my question. "Back to the Excelsior. It would seem that your attorneys called Reynolds. They warned him that you might come here claiming wild things about the past. I believe they called you unstable and in need of medication."

I stopped dead in my tracks, feeling my life could be unraveled in an instant. That cloud of doom hanging over me, blanketed me in a heartbeat. By one phone call, the illusion labeling me a "nut case in need of an asylum" had been created. And I had played into it over the years. By trying to conform to the expectations of my caretakers, by seeing the doctors, and by allowing pills to be prescribed even if I didn't take them, I'd left myself vulnerable.

What would it eventually be? An overdose like Meryl? A leap from Excelsior's tower? Or perhaps I'd drown in a fountain. "I'm not going anywhere. Not with you. Not with anyone. I've no wish to die."

Lance whipped around, surprise and then anger blazing in his gaze. He marched toward me. I stepped back a bit, but could go no further, when the reception desk hit my spine.

"Miss, are you all right?" The lady behind the desk asked. "Do you need help?"

I didn't look her way. My attention was riveted on Lance's anger and passion. He kept coming at me. He planted his hands on the desk behind me, trapping me in the circle of his arms. Leaning down, he kissed me, hard. His lips claimed mine firmly as he pressed his body into mine. I dropped my overnight bag and clung to his sides. His tongue slid between my lips and demanded a response that thrust me from any comfort zone I'd ever known.

In a tangled dance of give and take, he opened an erotic door that I wanted to rush through. My heart raced and my thoughts scrambled.

The kiss ended as abruptly as it had begun. Lance's gaze had gained a sensual edge but the anger still lurked. "Invitation accepted, Hani. The only thing you'll experience from my hands is pure pleasure. And *la petite mort* will be the only death delivered. Don't doubt me. I don't know what is going on or why, but I believe you, okay?"

"Oh, my! Just... oh my," the woman at the desk said.

I sucked in air. We'd created quite a scene.

"Are we good?" Lance asked. "If you need more convincing, we can get a room right here, right now. And not meet with anyone until you're ready."

"Take the room, honey," the woman at the desk said. "Lightning doesn't strike often."

He arched a brow and grinned. His cockiness was back and I had to admit it felt good, a familiarity in him that I'd known when I was younger, and trusted now. I thought about saying Lance wasn't a bolt out of the blue, but a nuclear power plant. Then decided it wasn't sophisticated enough. I also wondered what *la petite mort* meant, but decided to ask at a less public moment.

"We're good," I managed to stammer.

"Cool. Let's go tackle this beast then."

In the past, whenever there'd been a seemingly impossible motorcycle jump or trick he wanted to conquer, he always called it a beast. He grabbed my overnight bag, and this time, eased a hand to my back to usher me out.

"Come back later for that room. I've a honeymoon suite open." The woman at the desk called out after them. Lance gave her a

69

thumbs up sign, his blue eyes gleaming with humor and interest.

Outside, reality hit. It was nasty and teeming with a dangerous edge. The storms had moved in and chased away all but a few distant tourists, braving the storm by taking their pictures near the Sands marquee. Thick, heavy drops of rain plastered the sidewalk and created a foggy steam.

The bellboy motioned for a taxi, but a black Impala pulled up and a tinted window rolled down. A man grabbed me from behind and pressed the barrel of a gun to my side. "Get in," the man told Lance.

Keeping his grip on my bag, Lance held up his hands. The man shoved the gun harder against my ribs. I winced. "I won't tell you again. Get in."

The bellman cried out and ran toward the entrance. Someone in the car shot him in the back.

I met Lance's gaze with a silent "no" skewing my lips. Getting in that car would be like crawling into a coffin. I couldn't do it. I didn't want to be shot either. The only thing holding me upright were my wobbling knees, and I just let them go, went totally limp and fell back against the gunman as if I'd fainted. I slipped from his hold and he lost his balance.

I'm not sure what happened next. All I know is a split second later, Lance was on top of me, face buried in my chest. The echoes of more gunshots rang in my ears. The pouring rain outside the covered entry splattered my legs with a chilling mist, and the gunman who'd taken me hostage was out cold on the ground. My overnight bag lay near his head and the imprint of its designer logo dented in the middle of his forehead. Security men rushed from the hotel. The bellboy, though still on the ground, yelled for the security to call the police. He described the black Impala and even knew the license plate number.

"Are you hurt?" I ran my hands over his back, searching, pressing, determined to assure myself that he'd escaped unscathed.

He lifted his head and grinned. "That was an Oscar-winning faint. If the journalism gig doesn't work out, you might want to keep that in mind."

"I doubt my heart would survive the drama."

"Considering the way it seems to follow your wake, I'd thought you'd be used to it by now. You're going to tell me you still don't know those goons or what's going on?"

"I think I've told you everything I know. Honestly."

"Then maybe it's time for my attorney to have a talk with your attorney. If they're already out to malign you, then they know more than they're saying." He pushed up from the ground, then held out his hand for mine. Gaining my feet, I held firmly onto his arm. My knees shook more now than they had at gunpoint. He didn't wait for the police. He told the security boss to send the police to the Excelsior if they wanted to see him or examine the overnight bag he'd nailed the gunman with. The gunman, now hog-tied, was just waking up as we ducked into a taxi.

For the second time that day, after dreaming of Excelsior last night and my father's fall to his death, I entered the hotel, this time through a private entrance in the back where security men met Lance. They escorted us up to the Van Rathum's penthouse and stood guard outside of the double doors.

Memories washed over me, none of them good. In some ways, I came close to feeling like the grief-stricken girl again. I saw myself waking up, anxious about the day. Meryl's unexpected death still heavy in my heart and consuming my waking thoughts. I'd gone in search of my father. The moment I entered his room, I knew something was wrong. I felt the heat of the morning heavy in the room, coming from the open balcony door. Calling my father's name, I stepped outside. It was empty, but a chair had been turned on its side near the railing. I righted it, peered over the side, and saw the broken glass of the atrium near the pool below. In a numb state, I rushed downstairs and found my father's body. I'd been kneeling in the glass, cutting my hands and knees as I desperately tried to wake my father, when Arthur Van Rathum found me and brought me here. Arthur and Jena Vive had decorated their home as they imagined King Arthur might have done so. Suits of armor stood guard in the hallway and weaponry decorated the walls. There were pictures of knights and ladies everywhere. Even the dining room table had been custom built to look like the fictitious Round Table of the chivalrous, legendary knights.

"Maria? Reynolds?" Lance called out.

"In your father's office. We're having tea."

Tea? In Las Vegas?

We entered and Lance introduced me to the housekeeper and

Mr. Reynolds, both silver haired and distinguished. They made afternoon tea look perfectly normal. Lance's father sat in a chair close to the door. He had a magician's red silk scarf in his hands. He kept running his fingers over the silk, whispering something akin to abracadabra. Lance's loving and pain-filled glance in his father's direction was heartbreaking. The sadness of the broken and lost lives washed over me. So much tragedy had fallen over the past ten years.

Lance ushered me to a chair and sat in the adjoining one. He spoke forcefully. "Let me get directly to the point, Reynolds. Two men just tried to kidnap Miss Valentine and me in front of the Sands."

Maria cried out in horror, her teacup clattered loudly before she planted it on the coffee table. Reynold's gasped, turning white behind his wire-rimmed glasses.

Lance continued. "Apparently, there are people willing to kill to keep something secret. Do you know what it could be about? Did my father ever mention anything that Hans Valentine might have been worried about? Hannity believes what happened is tied to the past and something her father knew."

Reynold's glanced toward Arthur Van Rathum. "Your father never said anything specific, but after Mr. Valentine's death, he was gravely upset and gave me an envelope. It was to be opened should anything untoward happen to him."

Lance exploded from his chair. "You didn't think this important enough to tell me?"

Reynolds winced. "Legally, I can't. Nothing of a nefarious nature has happened."

Running his finger through his dark hair, Lance paced across the office. "Let me say this simply and once. My father had no way of knowing dementia would steal his mind away. He put you in charge of important information. Harm has come to him and we need to know what that information is."

Reynolds sighed and buried his head in his hands, his reply was muffled. "It only says to unlock the unlockable."

"What?" Lance marched toward him.

Mr. Reynold's raised his head. "When your father lost his mind completely, I opened the envelope. The piece of paper inside says to unlock the unlockable."

Lance smacked his hands together and I jumped up in

excitement. We spoke at the same time. "The magic box!"

"Where is it?" I asked.

"My father's room," Lance said. "When he first developed signs of losing his memory, he'd put the box under his bed. I thought he needed it close for comfort."

We all looked toward Lance's father, but Arthur wasn't in his chair.

"Dad?" Lance rushed from the room. I ran behind him and plowed into his back when he came to a quick stop.

Mr. Luca had a gun to Arthur's head. "Do you know how many years I've wasted waiting to find the tapes that bitch stole? It may be too late for anything else, but at least Sammy will go to his grave happy that bitch didn't get one over on him." He motioned to Lance. "You tie everyone here to a chair at the dinner table. If you behave, it will go quick for everyone. You try anything, and you have plenty of time to regret it as they burn to death. *Slowly*. And just so you know, my men replaced your men outside. Anyone but me walks out of here, and they'll put a bullet in your brain."

Strangely, I wasn't surprised to see Mr. Luca. I'd never trusted him.

Maria cried out and Reynolds wrapped her in his arms. "I've got you, Maria. Hold on to me." His tone was one of deep affection.

"Is Mr. Giovanni part of this?" I asked.

Mr. Luca laughed. "That ass doesn't know himself from a hole in the ground."

"But I do know shit when I smell it," Mr. Giovanni said, appearing with a pistol pointed at the back of Mr. Luca's head. "And I've had to smell it for a long time thanks to you."

Mr. Luca twisted, trying to thrust Arthur between him and Mr. Giovanni. "Who the hell are you?"

"FBI. A Cooper man through and through." Mr. Giovanni shot Mr. Luca between the eyes. Blood and gray matter splattered the wall.

Arthur fell to the floor, along with Mr. Luca's lifeless body. FBI or not, I knew it wasn't good for us that we'd witnessed Mr. Luca's demise. Lance didn't hesitate to react. He went low and ran headfirst at Mr. Giovanni. "Duck, Hannity," Lance yelled.

Mr. Giovanni aimed the pistol right at Lance. All I could think to do was grab an axe from the closest suit of armor and throw it at the man. It accomplished a miracle. Mr. Giovanni looked up at the projectile. His shot at Lance went awry and the axe hit the wall and clattered to the floor next to Mr. Giovanni's feet. Lance head-butted the man in the gut, then picked up the axe from the floor. Before Mr. Giovanni could aim, Lance slammed the flat side of the axe against the man's head. The man went down hard. Lance tied up Mr. Giovanni and collected the men's guns.

I locked the entry door, assuring no more gunmen could get in. Then I helped a confused Arthur to his feet. He patted my hand. "You're a dear. So glad you're all right. Hans would be proud."

Shocked, I blinked at the tears suddenly flooding my eyes. Arthur looked around. "Maria, have you seen Jena Vive? She should be back by now."

Lance groaned. Maria left Reynold's embrace and took Arthur by the hand. "I think it's time for you to take a rest now."

"Yes, a rest would be good." Arthur went with Maria.

Reynolds sank into a chair, his body shaking. "To think all of these years those murders were right there. *Good God*, they had almost total control over your life, Miss Valentine."

I'd suspected the dark cloud of death, but what just happened rattled me to my soul. Lance and I stood staring at each other.

"If the FBI man was on the wrong side of the law, then do we dare call the police?" I asked.

Lance nodded. "We'll call the press at the same time. They'll come with cameras and document everything. First, I think we need to open the magic box and see what this is all about."

Lance retrieved the box and quickly maneuvered the sliding wood until he unlocked the box. Inside were tapes, a typed transcript of what was on the tapes, and a note from Meryl.

She had stolen the tapes from Sam the Boss, head of the Giovanni crime family. The tapes proved that Jay Allen Cooper, the director of the FBI for almost fifty years, hired Sam the Boss to assassinate President Kincaid. Meryl and my father had been killed because of it. Why Arthur hadn't been killed remained a mystery. We called the police and the press, making as sure as we could that the truth would reach the light of day. We'd see what happened when the government got wind of the scandal.

What happened had me wondering who else had been assassinated by Cooper over the years. My journalistic curiosity couldn't wait to investigate, but I didn't mention it yet. Lance looked as if he needed a break. His hair stuck out in every direction. His cool manner appeared completely undone.

Someday, more truths would unravel the false illusions of the past. Some would believe that a sinister evil had lurked beneath our red, white and blue-bannered lives. Others would not. They would cling to their memories of the world they believed in.

"Thank *God*, Valentine is at camp," Lance said.

I nodded, knowing too well the trauma violence caused. "I'm looking forward to meeting her. I have been alone for so long." I shivered and the narrow escape I'd made from a tragic end.

Lance crossed the room, raking his hand through his hair. "When I think of what could have happened to you... thank *God* you came here for answers. As Reynolds said, those killers had you in their grip for years." He pulled me into his arms. He was warm and strong, and wonderfully male. "Hannity Valentine, what am I going to do with you?"

I pressed closer to him, so very thankful that we were alive and the truth had been found. "I believe I need enlightening on a few things."

He arched a brow. "Only a few?"

"Maybe more." I rose to my toes, pressing my breasts against his chest and whispered into his ear. "Can you explain what *la petit mort* means?"

"First, I will tell you. Then I will show you many, many times. It begins with a seduction. The gift of flowers and a shared smile."

"Like the bouquet you gave me from the magic box years ago? I still have the petals pressed in the pages of my diary."

"Yes, just like that. Only this time, instead of saying 'flowers for a forever Valentine,' I'd say 'flowers for *my* forever Valentine.' Then we would begin to explore our senses together. A fine meal, wine, music. I'd have you in my arms just like this and we'd begin a sensual dance. I'd kiss you like this."

He leaned down and slowly brought his mouth to mine. This time the fire he ignited flamed hotter and brighter than ever. My heart thundered in my chest and my insides melted. After the kiss, he continued to tell me exactly how he would undress me, just where he would touch me, and how he would make me feel, until I fainted from the pure pleasure of it all.

Breathless from just imaging it all, I whispered, "You're my magic man."

I held him close, vowing to never let the precious gifts of love, of passion, or of trust, to go unappreciated. I had found a new future. While not completely free of the past, a beautiful new world had opened for me to explore.

Tonight I would dream of love and live the promise of it with Lance's every kiss.

And tomorrow, I'd investigate another adventure for us to share.

5

COMING HOME

Kimberly Cates

1967

The last place in the world Grace Kilcannon wanted to be was Las Vegas, but she had to find Mike Wakefield before her brother Devin sneaked out of his hospital bed and Army-crawled all the way from Iowa City to the Excelsior Hotel.

"I might as well have walked across the desert myself, the way my feet hurt," she muttered, her left heel rubbed as raw as her nerves. She'd been traipsing from hotel to hotel on foot for what seemed an eternity without finding a trace of her twin's best friend.

She winced at the blast of a car horn, the flashing lights and bustle of people so different from her home back on her grandmother's farm. A world full of cornfields, haymows and the sleepy kind of peace Mike and Devin couldn't wait to leave behind when they'd shipped out for Vietnam three years ago. Grace's heart squeezed at the memory, Devin with his always-mussed auburn hair shaved in a military cut, and Mike, suddenly a stranger, indigo eyes watching her with the same wary tiger look he'd had when social services had dropped him off at a neighboring farm ten years ago. He'd been one more surly thirteen-year-old in a line of "last chance" foster kids Clem and Carol McGinty refused to give up on.

But Mike was one success the McGintys wouldn't claim. "Even the McGintys say it was fate Devin and I were up on their barn roof helping Granddad patch a leak when you arrived, Mike," Grace said under her breath, all too aware of how many times she'd fought with Mike in her head since he'd been gone.

Her hand tightened on her purse strap as she remembered that day. Devin had taken one look at Mike, slid down the thick rope that stretched from the haymow to the goat shed and landed at Mike's feet with a thump. From that moment Devin Kilcannon and Mike Wakefield had been inseparable. And Grace had rarely been more than a step behind them.

Grace had felt abandoned the day she watched the two friends load their duffle bags into the luggage compartment of the bus that would carry them away. Together. Of course together. The two of them were part of the Navy's newly commissioned SEAL team, because just going to war as a soldier wasn't dangerous enough to satisfy the daredevil tendencies they'd always shared.

Tendencies Grace had shared too, Mike had pointed out just before he boarded the bus that day.

"You were worse than Devin and me once upon a time, Gracie May. From the time we opened that package from my dad and found that old sword, you were always diving in the middle of things, saber drawn. I miss that girl."

"I miss her too," Grace thought. That Gracie May hadn't learned how to be afraid. But five years of watching her family's farm slide closer to foreclosure had worn away at her confidence. Not to mention the biggest disaster of all—her stupid stunt of falling in love with Mike and telling him so. Three days later Mike had enlisted in the Navy, and Dev announced he wasn't about to stay home and let Mike have all the fun.

"Now Devin is missing a leg and Mike is... missing." Grace bit her lip, not sure which man's circumstance hurt her heart more.

It had been a real kick in the stomach to realize that Mike had been discharged from the Navy, stopped in at the McGintys' farm overnight, but hadn't even bothered to phone Dev and let him know he was stateside. If one of the McGintys' new foster kids hadn't spilled the news when they were visiting Dev at the Veteran's Hospital, Devin would never have known. And Grace wouldn't be trudging along the Vegas Strip, dreading the prospect of coming face to face with the man who had run half way across the world the moment she told him she loved him.

The hot Nevada wind gusted through the crowded streets, blowing Grace's long red hair into her face. She swiped the strands back over her shoulder then rubbed her palm against her peacock blue skirt. She could almost feel her brother's fingers clutching hers.

"He blames himself for what happened to me," Dev had told her. "Thinks you blame him too."

"Yeah, well, I do," Grace said. "If the shoe fits... "

"I'll only be needing one shoe for the moment." Devin forced a grin.

She'd looked down at the footrests on the wheelchair he was sitting in. The terrible empty spot where his left foot should have been.

"C'mon Grace," Devin had pressed her. "You know you're the only one who can talk to Mike when he's like this."

"Maybe a long time ago. Not anymore." There had been a time she and Mike had never run out of things to talk about. Especially when he'd been angry or frustrated or stalked by memories of the vagabond years he'd spent with his father in Las Vegas. But she'd never heard a silence more deafening than the one that had followed that fateful night near Sauk Lake.

Devin had grimaced. "Hell, Grace. Mike told me all about what happened. Think he was hoping I'd get so mad I'd stay alive long enough to knock him six ways to Sunday. Now I'll have to beat him with my wooden leg like that guy in the stories you used to tell us in the tree fort."

She must have looked appalled.

"It was a joke, Grace. Remember. That pirate guy... Captain Dirty Bird."

How could she forget? She'd loved the sensation of having an audience in her power, drawing out the tension, then at the most exciting moment, going off to bed, leaving the heroes she'd invented dangling over a pit full of vipers or tunneling under a castle wall, trapped as the soldiers of the watch traipsed near.

Devin had begged for more. But Mike had been different—she'd known he would spend the night in McGinty's hayloft, imagining ways to get her heroes free. Had he been craving adventures like the ones in her stories? Was that what had spurred him to join the SEALs? The thought had made her stomach clench as the leaf-green scents of childhood summers were lost in the astringent smells of the hospital. She turned back to her brother.

"I don't even know where to start looking for Mike," she insisted.

"Vegas." Devin paled when he said it, no longer able to hide his unease.

The nape of Grace's neck prickled. "Mike's not in Vegas. He swore he'd never go back there."

Once, when they'd scored a bottle of Boone's Farm Strawberry Hill wine from some local college kids, Mike had told them about his years growing up in Vegas, following his gambler pop around to the casinos until Bob Wakefield's luck had run out and he'd turned Mike over to some cousin in Iowa so the kid could eat. Mike had kicked up as much trouble as possible, figuring the family would send him back to his dad. Instead, he'd ended up in foster care. His old man had sent him the sword along with a note saying he was sorry. If the package had come to any of his other foster homes, they would have notified the authorities and got rid of the thing. A foster kid with anger issues and a sword—well, not exactly a scenario that made even the best foster parents get a good night's sleep.

But the McGintys had kept it safe for him, let him take it out when he asked. "Grace, Mike came back for the sword," Dev had told her. "He pawned it."

Her stomach had knotted. "He wouldn't do that!" It was his one link to his family and the history his mom had tracked down in genealogy before she died. He had no memories of her, except the carefully inscribed notes and stories about a sword and the people who had used it. Jacobite lords, Cavalier ladies captured in a tale she called Crown of Mist.

What force could possibly drive Mike to sell his most precious possession? Grace winced, remembering Mike joking around. *Pop was full of great advice*, he'd said. *Showed me how to get up on a rooftop once. Said: Gotta know where to jump if you lose it all, kid.*

No. Mike wouldn't do anything so crazy, would he? Even after what had happened to Devin? Even if he blamed himself? He'd have to know that Devin needed him more than ever. Or would her brother just get left behind now, the way she had when her love had threatened to slow Mike Wakefield down?

Devin had handed her a list of the hotels and casinos Mike's father had frequented, saying that it was a place to start. Could Mike be looking for his dad? Going somewhere familiar? He'd said the chorus girls were kind to him when he was a kid.

But he wasn't a sullen little boy anymore. He'd have gorgeous chorus girls lining up to watch him throw perfectly good money away on the turn of a card. She didn't want to think about how badly she and Devin would need that money before her brother could come home. The farmhouse had been built before the Civil War. It was about as wheelchair accessible as a fun house at the County Fair.

"Hey, watch it, lady!" The sharp cry startled her as a man in a cowboy hat nearly jostled her into the street. "Got to keep your wits about you, honey. Everyone in Vegas is in a hurry to get to their next good time!"

Everyone except me, Grace thought, forcing herself toward the Excelsior's entrance. "You're not going to find Mike standing out here," she muttered to herself. "Go in and cross another hotel off of your list."

Sucking in a deep breath, she swept through the door.

The Excelsior even smelled like big money—fine leather, expensive cologne, the scent from bouquets of flowers set strategically about the lobby. Bright lights gleamed, jewels flashed. Powerful men strode about, garbed in expensive suits and recklessness. Here and there clusters of hotel guests gathered, having a good time. A couple with T-shirts that said Bride and Groom were cuddled together on one of the leather sofas. Grace saw the man kiss his new wife's ear, and a pretty flush spread across the bride's cheeks. There had been a time she'd imagined a honeymoon with Mike, a wedding night.

"Can I help you?" a front desk clerk asked her.

She'd learned early that she needed a ruse to find out if a guest was registered. "I'm supposed to meet Sergeant Michael Wakefield for dinner here in the lobby. I'm afraid I got the wrong hotel."

"Oh, no. Right hotel. I saw him at the blackjack table a while ago."

She gripped the counter. He hadn't jumped.

She hadn't really believed he could do such a thing, had she? So why did she feel such relief? In an instant, fury rushed through her. Grace charged into the casino. It should have been easy to see Mike in the crowd. At six foot five he was a head taller than most of the other men in the room. Besides which, from the time they were kids, he'd pulled at her, like a compass needle. Michael Wakefield had been her true north.

She saw him bending over a leggy blond cocktail waitress, saying something in her ear to be heard above the buzzers and bells and chatter. The woman pushed up on tiptoe and kissed him full on the mouth. Was it jealousy that made a red haze of rage descend over her? Or the fact that Mike was here, having a good time, while everyone who loved him was worried sick—so worried Devin had sent her rushing halfway across the country to chase after him.

Good thing Mike hadn't jumped, Grace thought. She'd get the pleasure of pushing him off a cliff herself.

She cut through the crowd of hotel guests, nearly tipping over a tray of martinis and avoiding men trying to catch her attention. Mike didn't even notice her approach until she got close enough to slug him in the arm.

Pain shot through her hand on impact.

In an instant, Mike had whipped the waitress behind him, and caught hold of Grace's wrist. She could see the tension in him, the readiness for a fight.

His eyes widened in surprise for a moment as he registered that he'd been accosted by a woman.

"Whoa there, beautiful! What the... ?"

She knew the instant he recognized her. His brows crashed low over his piercing eyes, his chiseled features wolf-like and sharp. A warrior's face. It wasn't hard to imagine the Jacobite ancestor Mike had been named for, wielding the dragon-sword they'd spun so many stories about.

"Grace?" he said, a dull flush rising up his throat to his cheeks. He shook his head, as if to clear his vision. "What the hell are you doing here?"

"Who's this, sugar?" the leggy blonde said in a southern drawl. "She doesn't look very happy to see you."

"Oh, I'm happy to see him, all right. In fact, I'm just thrilled he hasn't jumped off a roof somewhere. It gives me the pleasure of shoving him off of one myself."

"That red hair's no lie," the woman laughed. "I'm Candace. Mikey and I used to hang out when our dads—"

"I'll catch up with you later, Candace," Mike said, tugging at the collar of his blue pinstriped shirt. "I need to find out what's going on here." He grasped Grace by the elbow. She tried to yank away, but couldn't escape his grip as he steered her through the noisy crowd. At last he maneuvered her into the shade of a potted palm, far enough from the chaos that voices couldn't be heard. "Grace, is something wrong with Devin?"

"Yeah. He's lost his leg, and his best friend breezed into town and took off without so much as a phone call."

Mike's eyes turned cool. "There wasn't time. I had some business to take care of."

"You had time to stop at McGinty's. You had time to pawn your sword. It would have taken fifteen minutes to stop by and see Dev. To call him. He was ready to check himself out of the hospital and come chasing after you."

"Why would he do that?"

"He was scared you were going to jump off a roof or something."

Mike's brow furrowed. "A roof?"

"Yeah. He found out you'd pawned the sword."

Mike's jaw tightened. "How did that happen? No one was supposed to know."

"Well, the McGintys *did* visit Dev and brought one of the new foster kids with them. The kid blurted out the whole story. Nothing more fun than blowing the lid off of someone else's secret when you're determined to prove what a rotten kid you are. Maybe you remember when you went through that stage. I sure do."

A memory flashed in her mind, Mike pocketing a candy bar in Wilson's gas station. She'd made him put it back.

"Devin was afraid you were going off the rails again," she snapped. "That you felt guilty since you were the one who got him to enlist. Now he's lost a leg... "

"I'm not going off the rails." Michael angled his face into the shadow, paused a moment, then said, "As for the Navy—Devin's a grown man. He made his own choices."

Something in his tone of voice infuriated her. "You can't even

83

look me in the eye." Her hands balled into fists. "You know he never would have joined up if it weren't for you. And he told us all about how he followed you into the SEALs training."

Mike's eyes narrowed, some emotion she couldn't name sparking beneath his dark lashes. "Devin told you that? Or was it just easier for you to think that he did? One more reason to stop loving me?"

The words jolted her. He was watching her, eyes shuttered in his ruggedly handsome face.

Grace drew herself up, determined not to let him see the scars he'd left. "You think I spent three years making myself miserable over you? It was a stupid teenage infatuation that ended us up in the back seat of a Buick and then fell apart when the sun came up." She choked out a laugh. "You really didn't have to run all the way to Vietnam, Mike. I was smart enough to realize it was a mistake pretty quick on my own."

"You've obviously got everything all figured out." Mike crossed his arms over his broad chest. How dare he look at her like *she* was the jerk?

"You couldn't face me after we had sex. You can't face Dev now that he's in a wheelchair. Hard to maneuver one around a place like this." Grace gestured to the crowded room. "Besides, I'd imagine girls like Candace don't like the inconvenience." She wished the words back the minute they slipped out.

Mike had always been able to read people better than anyone Grace had ever known. "Candace and I knew each other when we were kids. That's all. Though why I'm explaining myself to you, I have no idea," his voice hardened. "There's nothing between you and me, right? It was all a stupid mistake."

People were starting to stare. Even the bride and groom she'd seen earlier had turned to see what the commotion was.

Mike ran his hand through his hair. She ached at the familiar gesture, remembering how silky the dark strands had felt sliding between her fingers. How Mike's skin had heated when she touched him, how his breath caught when she'd unbuttoned his shirt.

We can't do this, Gracie May. I swore I'd take care of you.

How was he going to do that when he was off at college, earning his full-ride scholarship quarterbacking at ISU all the way across the state in Ames? She'd wanted him to know what he meant to her, before the chance to tell him slipped away. She'd sensed in him the empty place, a home that wasn't, a family that should have been. A father who was more like a friend, a mother he'd never known. Had anyone ever told Michael Wakefield that they loved him?

Was Mike thinking of that day too?

Grace swallowed hard. "Listen, I have to find a payphone, let Devin know that I found you."

He kneaded the muscles in his neck. Grace remembered when she used to do it for him after football games. How his head would droop and his eyes drift closed.

"You can use the phone in my room," Mike said, letting his hand fall to his side. "It's private. No need for everyone in Vegas to overhear what a jerk I am."

"That's okay. I'd rather—"

"You're limping and you look like you walked all the way from Iowa."

Grace shifted, unnerved that he'd noticed. She'd been so stressed by seeing Mike again that she'd forgotten how much her feet hurt. Now, once again, she could feel every blister.

Mike's mouth curved in that half-smile that still made her heart turn over.

"I'm hardly going to fling you down onto my bed and have my way with you," he said. "We're over that little spate of insanity, right? I'll grab a bottle of pop for you while you talk to Devin. You've got to be thirsty."

She suddenly realized her mouth was bone dry. She couldn't imagine how good it would feel to kick off her boots. Maybe while Mike was gone she could scrounge a Band Aid out of her purse and put it on the place where she could feel the damp spot from a burst blister.

"After you're done telling Dev I'm fine, I'll buy you dinner," he said with a frown. "It's the least I can do since it's my fault you had to drag yourself all the way from Iowa."

For a moment, pride almost won out. She almost told him to forget it. Then she thought about all the expenses she was facing when Devin got out of the hospital. Mr. McGinty had volunteered to build a ramp so Dev could get his wheelchair up the stairs that led to the farmhouse's big front porch, but once they got Dev into the house, then what? The doors were too narrow, the stairs leading up to the second floor and the bedrooms loomed, treacherously steep.

Grace blinked back tears as she thought of her brother's room, still just the way he'd left it when he and Mike had shipped out. The abandoned hornet's nest he and Mike had found hanging from a tree branch was wired to the ceiling. His Boy Scout sash hung over his desk chair, sunlight filtering through the curtains grandma had sewn. Cowboys printed against a garish sunset orange. No matter how old Dev got, he wouldn't change them. Said it was like Grandma was still in the room with him.

And on Dev's desk, a picture of Mike, Devin and Grace—arms looped around each other's shoulders while they grinned like loons, a waterfall on the Eau Claire River in Wisconsin behind them. They'd just jumped off the outcropping of rock above them and splashed into the river, letting the current from the waterfall carry them down a second, smaller fall, the rushing water sweeping them along like a rollercoaster. That was the day Grace had realized she was in love with Mike. Every time she looked at him, she felt that same wild rollercoaster sensation in her chest.

"Grace?" Mike touched her arm, his voice suddenly tender, reminding her of other times, all the times when something had hurt her, like when mean girls in high school mocked the clothes her grandma had sewn for her to save money. *You're worth a dozen of those girls, Grace. You know what it means to have a grandma who loves you.*

And then her beloved collie had gone missing, Mike had searched all night, and had carried Shep home in his arms. The dog had tangled with some other critter, and while the vet stitched Shep up, Mike had held Grace in his arms. She'd cried, and he'd murmured against her hair. *Hush, Gracie May, you don't have to worry anymore. I'm always gonna take care of you.*

She'd believed him. Grace blinked back tears. How had they ended up here—strangers in this Vegas hotel?

"Come on, Trouble," Mike said, using the childhood nickname her grandma had given her. "You look beat. Time to set down the weight of the world."

He slipped his arm around her. She didn't want to be grateful, but it had been so long since anyone had hugged her, taken care of her, even for a little while. He guided her to the elevator and they whisked up to the eighth floor. The hallway was deserted. He led her to his room, then keyed the lock and pushed the door open. Then he left her alone.

The telephone sat on a desk that was scattered with papers. Grace sagged down on the desk chair, and picked up the phone. She dialed, waited for long distance to connect her.

There was a flurry on the other end, hospital attendants going off to find Dev, bring him to the phone. She tugged off her boots and sighed in relief, wiggling her toes, letting the cooler air soothe her hot, tired feet.

"Gracie?" Devin's voice sounded a million miles away. The line crackled, but she could hear the fear in his voice.

"I found Mike. He was gambling at the Excelsior. He's fine."

She heard Devin heave a gusty sigh. "Thank God you found him. But, Gracie, he's not *fine*."

"He is," she insisted, twisting the phone cord around her finger. "He'd been playing blackjack and flirting with some woman named Candace from the old days he spent here as a kid."

"I don't care what he told you, or what you want to believe. Mike's not fine," Devin insisted. "He pawned the sword, Grace. He didn't come to see me. Mike doesn't ditch people he loves."

"Well, I wouldn't know." Grace pushed to her feet, pacing as far as the phone cord would allow. "Mike enlisted in the Navy days after I told him I loved him. Couldn't wait to get away."

"About that," Devin said slowly. "I think it's time I told you... well, I was the one who enlisted."

"I know." She moved toward the window, looking north across the skyline, toward Iowa and home. "You couldn't let Mike have all the fun without you," she said, bitter.

"Mike didn't want me to go."

Grace was sure she'd heard him wrong. "What did you say?"

"Mike told me I was being an ass. Said you needed me on the farm. That you already had enough to worry about."

"That much was true." She had worked herself to the point of exhaustion trying to keep the place running on her own.

"Grace, I signed up in spite of what Mike said." Devin's voice grew gravelly with regret. "Then I didn't have the guts to look you in the face and tell you that I did it. Felt like such a selfish bastard, so I lied. Told you Mike had signed up first."

Grace's hand tightened on the phone. "He didn't?"

"No."

She sank down on the corner of the bed, feeling dazed. "But the

SEALs. He volunteered for hazardous duty."

"I started that rodeo as well."

Anger pricked her, but hadn't Devin already paid a terrible price?

"You know I could never stand it when Mike beat me in anything," Devin explained. "At least I was a stronger swimmer than he was. Or so I thought. The guy doesn't know the meaning of the word quit. He practically killed himself, but damn if he didn't make the team."

"That doesn't change the fact that he left after I told him I loved him," she insisted, more to herself than to Devin. "After we—"

"Don't you think it's time you asked Mike why?"

She started to protest, but her gaze caught on the nightstand. She went still. A battered frame had been placed there, a jagged crack in the glass. She'd never seen the photo it contained.

Mike must have snapped it that day at the Eau Claire River. She was frozen, mid-leap from the stone outcropping, her face lit up with excitement. A wild, brave water sprite in a moment of perfect freedom. Before her world caved in.

She didn't know how long she'd stared at the photo before Devin spoke.

"Listen, sis, I've gotta go. This pretty nurse here is insisting it's time for physical therapy."

"Devin—"

"I'm sorry I was such a coward about telling you about the Navy stuff. I never should've let Mike take the heat. I didn't know about, well, the feelings you had for each other."

"We didn't have feelings for each other. It was all me. A high school thing."

"Huh. And people always said you were the smart twin." Devin cleared his throat, his voice thick with emotions she knew he was trying to hide. "Gotta go, buffalo," he said with forced lightness.

Grace's eyes stung. Devin had started making up funny ways to say goodbye when they'd started kindergarten and hadn't wanted to let go of his hand.

"See you later, Devin-gator." The phone clicked, the line went dead. She crossed to the desk to put the handset back into the cradle, then tried to digest everything her brother had told her. She'd been blaming Mike for so long—for everything that had gone wrong. Devin joining the Navy and getting hurt. Her own broken heart.

She'd felt used, rejected. So let down when he left her. She closed her eyes, remembering his rough voice as he learned her body by touch the night they'd made love. *Promised I'd take care of you...*

She heard footsteps coming down the hall, the key turning the lock's tumblers. Mike walked in, balancing an orange soda and a tray with two cheeseburgers and fries.

"Picked this up on my way," he said, setting the tray on the nightstand. "Figured you must be hungry. I know how you get when you're upset. You forget to eat."

"Yeah. I do." It felt so surreal—being in the room with Mike after so long, knowing that she couldn't blame him anymore, not knowing what that meant.

Mike nudged the tray toward her. "Extra pickles and extra ketchup, just the way you like it."

"Thanks." She reached for a fry then let her hand fall back to her side. No way she could swallow anything past the lump in her throat. "I talked to Devin," she said.

"Good." Mike popped a fry in his mouth "Dev knows I'm okay."

"Actually, no. You're not okay. At least, that's what he says."

Mike brushed some grains of salt off of his hand. "Grace, you can see for yourself. I'm fine. Crisis over."

Then why did she see so many secrets still hidden in his eyes? "I still don't know why you pawned the sword. I know how much you loved that thing. So does Devin."

Mike shrugged. "I needed a stake to gamble with. It's the only way I could make sure I had enough to put on the table."

"You've never been a gambler. Why start now? Why start so big? Pawning stuff you treasure... isn't that what your dad used to do?"

"Yeah. Well, guess I figured out there are some gambles worth taking." He crossed to the window and tugged it open, letting in the hot desert breeze. "I needed big money, fast."

"What for?"

He wheeled toward her. "Grace, Devin's got to come home from the hospital sometime. How the hell is he going to get around the farmhouse?"

She stiffened under the force of his gaze. "I've been worried about that myself."

"Well, you don't have to worry anymore." He grabbed a sheaf of papers and spread them across the desk. Blueprints. Estimates. Lists of contractors with Iowa addresses. "See, I had these plans drawn up by a guy I know—Navy buddy of mine who wants to join the family business and be an architect when he gets out. His dad looked the blueprints over. They're spot on. Grab bars wherever Dev might need them until he gets steady on his prosthesis. A lift to get him up those stairs to the bedrooms." He pointed to the drawing, his hand so strong and tan. A man's capable hand instead of the boy's hand that had been as familiar as her own.

"Mr. McGinty already volunteered to build a ramp to the front porch."

"Of course he did." Affection warmed Mike's face. "Clem is the best." Mike sobered. "Clem's not as young as he used to be, though. There are changes here beyond what he can do. Load bearing walls we have to consider. Dev's going to be back on his feet in no time— he's one hell of a fighter—but I figured if we could outfit the house, we could make the transition easier."

Grace tipped her head to one side, examining the blueprints before her. "You planned all this?"

"It's paid for too, as of tonight." Mike's chin tipped at a belligerent angle. "I had just cashed out when you came down on me like a Valkyrie." He chuckled. "You always were something to see when you were defending someone you love, Gracie May. I've never known anybody with a bigger heart."

Grace's chest ached. Was that really how Mike saw her?

"But you didn't want it. My heart," she said softly. "You joined the Navy."

Mike's hands knotted atop the house plans. He straightened up, turned away. She knew he was looking at the picture on the nightstand. "I'm real sorry about that, Grace," he said, low. "And about, well, Dev's leg. It's the least I can do, help you with the house, since he'd never have joined the SEALs if I hadn't."

"So you're saying it's all your fault. The fact that Devin joined the Navy. Went to Vietnam. Joined the SEALs. Came home missing a leg."

Mike winced. "I'd take his place in a second if I could."

"I know that you would." Grace hesitated, her throat tight. "But you didn't join the Navy first, Mike. And you weren't the one who jumped at the chance to train for hazardous duty, were you?"

Mike stiffened. He turned to face her, his eyes wary. "Sure, I did. I... "

"Devin told me the truth just now. It's about damned time."

"Oh." Mike gripped the back of the chair, his knuckles white.

"I'm sorry," Grace said, sitting down on the bed. "I'm sorry I blamed you. I'm sorry I didn't ever ask... I was just so hurt. It was easy to believe..." She plucked at her skirt, her fingers trembling.

Mike sat down beside her and covered her hand with his own. "What was easy to believe?" Mike prodded.

"That I'd ruined things," Grace confessed in a rush. "That you wanted to get out of town, as far away from me as you could, once I said... well... you know. You were there."

"I'm not likely to forget that night." His face tightened, and she could sense sadness in him, a loss she'd been too blind to see.

"Mike, Devin said I should ask you why you left. Maybe it's time I did."

For long moments he was silent, skimming his thumb over her knuckles. "I know what it's like to be without a family, Gracie May," he said, bleak with old pain. "Without someone who shares the same memories, who has to love you, to take you in, even when you're a jerk. Even when things get hard." His drew a deep breath. "You want to know why I enlisted with Dev? I couldn't stand the thought of you losing him, ending up alone like me."

Grace looked up at him, let her heart show in her eyes. Three years of missing Mike, even after he'd walked away.

"I told you I loved you." Her voice quavered. "You never said a word back."

"I was stunned," Mike said. "You know, no one ever said that to me. Mom died when I was too little to remember. Pop, well, he'd had a lot of tough knocks. It wasn't something guys like him said. I made it hard as hell for my foster parents to love me. That was supposed to make them send me back to my Pop."

Mike curled his finger under her chin, turning her face up to his. It was almost more than Grace could bear—the intensity of his eyes, so blue, so tender, his defenses stripped away.

"Then, there you were." Awe filled his voice. "Your hands on my skin, your mouth... you were so brave, so beautiful... telling me that you loved me. Hell, I couldn't speak. I couldn't breathe. I was so carried away all I could do was try to show you when we made love.

Make you feel what I couldn't say." He grasped her hands tight in his, holding on as if he'd never let her go. "That was the first time I got ready to pawn the sword. I wanted to buy you a ring. Ask you to wait for me while I went to college, studied so I could make a good life for you. For us. Then Devin enlisted and... well, my plans went to hell."

Grace's heart felt ready to beat its way out of her chest. "Why didn't you tell me? That you loved me? Why did you let me believe you walked away?"

"Chances were we were going to Vietnam. I'd seen what happened to men who went to war. Some came back maimed. Some died. All of them came back different. Changed from the men they were. I loved you too much to make you wait for a man who might never come back. You deserved to go to school, have fun, go to your college homecoming. I wouldn't be there to take you. But I failed you, Gracie May. I couldn't keep Devin from being wounded."

She couldn't bear the guilt that shadowed his face. She pressed her hand against his cheek, feeling the faint stubble along his jaw. Feeling all he'd sacrificed for her. What it had cost him. "Devin made his own choices, just like you told me. I'm sorry I wasn't listening."

A gust of wind blew through the open window, ruffling the papers on the desk. Instinctively, she dove to catch them. Her brow furrowed as she glimpsed something she hadn't seen before. A drawing far cruder than the ones his architect friend had made. "What's this?" she asked.

His cheeks darkened. "Uh, nothing. Just something I sketched out for myself."

"I know that place," Grace said, her pulse tripping. "That's where the tree fort is. Up on the hill. And this drawing is a floor plan."

Mike took the sketch, smoothed one of the creases in it. "The farmhouse is Dev's. I know your grandma left it to him."

"There's been a Kilcannon on that farm for two hundred years. She always figured I'd get married and change my name," Grace said.

"I thought maybe Dev would let me buy that patch of ground. Build a place of my own."

Pleasure bubbled in Grace at the thought of Mike living nearby.

"Devin will need help running the farm—what with his leg and all," she said, reminding herself that wanting to live near Devin didn't mean Mike wanted a life with her... still hope fluttered in her chest.

"I drew the plans before Devin got hurt," Mike told her. "I carried the sketch in my uniform pocket every day I was in Nam. Kept it sealed in plastic so it wouldn't get ruined. Kept it so I'd remember what I was fighting for."

"Home," Grace said, wishing with all her heart that he would have one at last.

"A home, yes," Mike said. "For us, if I could convince you to forgive me."

Her pulse raced.

"See this balcony?" He pointed to the drawing. "It's just off our bedroom. We could climb over the rail right into the old tree fort. I thought our kids could camp out at night there with Devin's kids, and you could tell them stories like the ones you told Dev and me. It used to drive me crazy, the way you'd leave us in suspense. The hero dangling over a volcano somewhere or his ship being boarded by pirates. Been feeling the same way ever since I left Iowa three years ago." Mike set the house plan aside and grasped her shoulders, turning her to face him. Her pulse tripped as he threaded his hands through her hair, tipping her face up to his.

What Grace saw in Mike's eyes made her heart feel as if it would beat its way out of her chest.

"Earlier you said you stopped loving me." Pain roughened his voice. "Did you, Grace? Stop?"

"I wanted to," Grace confessed. "I tried to. I kept myself so angry at you. Thinking what I'd say to you the next time we were face to face."

Mike chuckled, the sound so tender it made her chest ache. "You did a pretty good job of telling me what you thought of me when we were in the casino."

Grace's cheeks burned at the memory of how angry she'd been, how little she'd understood. "If I stayed mad at you, you'd come home," she tried to explain. "Crazy isn't it? But that's what I thought."

"Sometimes I think I loved you since the moment I saw you standing up on that barn roof the day I got dumped at McGintys'," Mike said, his voice hushed. "I didn't know much, Grace, but I knew how fiercely you loved the people in your life. I knew you'd fight for them. I wanted to fight for you." He brushed his thumbs across her cheeks, and she wanted to bury herself against him, but something held her back, an understanding of just how hard it was for him to put love into words. Knowing that he had more to say and that he'd never had anyone before, to love him this way, to listen.

"It's funny," he said after a long moment. "Those stories my mom wrote about the cavalier's sword. The engraving on it... the Latin... it said *I battle my own demons*. There was this crazy family legend that said the sword didn't belong to the cavalier, but was a gift to his lady. I thought it was ridiculous until I loved you." He raised his hand to her face, all their secrets laid bare. "You're the bravest person I know, and the most loving," Mike said, pressing a kiss to her brow. "You can slay your own demons, just like the cavalier's lady could, but I'd be proud if you'd let me stand with you. Marry me, Grace. Here. Now."

Grace flung herself against him, laughing, crying. "Wait!" she said after a moment. "You want to get married in Vegas?" She glanced out the window where the neon lights glowed. "This is the last place I'd ever imagined I'd get married."

"I've been waiting my whole life for you, Gracie May," Mike said. "Damned if I'll wait one more day."

Grace twined her arms around his neck and kissed him with all the love in her heart. Michael Wakefield was coming home at last.

6

BREATH OF LUCK

Tara Nina

Excelsior Hotel, Las Vegas, 1963

"Did you see?" Lolita twirled, giddily. Her signature full-length, silver gown fanned out at the bottom, dancing around her matching high heels. She practically squealed, breathlessly, "Sinatra was in the audience."

Luigi "Lucky" DiBonadetta closed the door behind him and simply stood quietly, staring at the most beautiful woman he'd ever known. The more she spun, the more her brilliant red curls bounced. He'd fallen in love the first moment he'd seen her, the day she'd auditioned for the lounge. Her voice was pure heaven laced with sexy seductress. Her beauty was only outmatched by her kind, loving nature. Being with her made him a better man and he didn't plan to lose her. He crossed the living area of the Sunrise Suite and captured Lolita in a warm hug. "This is only the beginning, my love. Word is Sinatra's creating a new show and was scouting local talent to open for him."

"You think he liked me?" She draped her arms around his neck as she smiled at him. When he hesitated to answer, she nibbled her lower lip—a nervous habit of hers that he found to be adorable.

"I *know* he loved you." He tapped her nose with his fingertip, lightly, then rested his hands at her waist. Intentionally, he let his gaze drift down the length of her body, then returned to her smoky gray eyes. "He'd have to be deaf not to. The Piano Lounge is packed every night you sing. Those people come to see you. He's a businessman, not a fool. He knows a good thing when he sees one."

"Oh, Lucky, I hope you're right." Her gray eyes seemed to shine, showing her excitement. He loved that about her. She couldn't hide her emotions from him. Lolita was full of joy and happiness, something he'd never known until she'd entered his world. If anyone deserved a break like this one, it was Lolita. In a business of clawing their way to the top, she wasn't that sort of bitch. She was a package of talent and class all rolled into a beautiful soul. Lucky's desire grew as she rubbed against him, making them both fully aware of their need for one another.

"I know I am." He felt her shiver in his arms as he leaned in and stole a long luxurious kiss, enjoying her taste before stepping out of their embrace. He crossed to the ornate French doors leading to the balcony and swung them open. "Let's have dinner overlooking our city of opportunity. Tonight is only the beginning."

A knock sounded on the door followed by a muffled announcement, "Room service."

He caught her elbow before she moved toward it. "I'll get that, babe. I ordered dinner and champagne to celebrate. Why don't you get comfortable?"

She kissed his cheek and scooted into the bedroom to change. Lucky opened the door then turned, motioning toward the French doors. "Please push the cart over to the balcony. My lady and I wish to dine under the stars."

"*Your* lady."

Lucky froze at the sound of the voice he'd grown to hate. He turned to face what he'd thought was a waiter from the kitchen. Instead, the person lifted her head, showing the face that had been hidden by a hat tugged low on her brow. There stood his venomous ex-wife.

"What do you want?"

"You know what I want, Lucky," she said. "I want you. I want the life we had before you became enchanted with that red-headed bitch."

"Dottie, we were over before I met her. Check the date on the divorce papers. They were signed months prior to Lolita entering my life. Don't blame our marriage ending on her."

"If she wasn't around, you'd still be mine," she spat out, drawing a gun from where she'd hidden it on the cart.

"What the hell! Dottie, put that away!" Lucky yelled.

"Lucky, what's going on?" Lolita asked, running into the room.

Dottie instantly switched targets and pulled the trigger. Lucky had Lolita in his arms before she hit the floor. Blood leaked from the wound in her chest, soaking her silver gown in crimson red.

"Lolita," Lucky gasped. "Oh my god. Stay with me, honey."

She coughed and sputtered. Blood leaked from the corner of her mouth. "Lucky," she whispered. "I love you." Her eyes closed and his heart shattered, instantly.

Lucky laid her gently on the floor, then sprang at Dottie. "You bitch!"

He fought her for the gun. It fired. The muzzle was pressed between them. He lowered to his knees, staring wide-eyed at her. Red seeped through his fingers as he held them against the hole in his stomach. Dottie's hands shook and the gun fell to the floor.

"Luigi, I never meant..." Tears streamed down her cheeks. "I wanted you back."

"You can't have me. You never truly did." He grabbed the gun, sank back on his heels and pointed it at her. "I love Lolita. I always will." He squeezed the trigger, hitting Dottie between the eyes. She was dead before she hit the floor.

Lucky wheezed in a breath, knowing he was dying. Blood oozed out. He coughed. He crawled to Lolita, pulling a ring box from his pocket. He reached for her as the last of his life trickled through his wound. His hand landed on hers, placing the box in her palm. Their dead-eyed gazes locked eternally on one another. The lovers were gone.

Excelsior Hotel, Las Vegas, 2015

"All we need is a hard eight, Jax, and we win big."

Jax held the dice in his hand. It had to be beginner's luck. It was his first time ever in a casino. He'd never played a game of craps before in his life and now he sat one roll away from a huge payout. According to the stickman working the table, it was the largest in weeks. His two best friends and business partners stood beside him, Arnie Adams on his right and Dennis Davison on the left. They'd come to Vegas to blow off steam from a frustrating workweek. Their company, Cooptown Diversions, designed Internet and video games. A lot was riding on their latest creation, which had been delayed from rolling out on time due to a couple of programming issues. Arnie claimed a trip away would help them de-stress and Vegas was where the dart landed when he threw it at the map on the wall in his office. They'd taken the redeye flight from JFK out of New York. Several times on the train ride into NYC from their company's base in Scarsdale, Jax almost talked himself out of going, but his friends had been persistent. Now, after a few hours of carefree sightseeing and gambling, he was more relaxed and on the verge of a major financial windfall.

He looked at the squares, red and white, numbered items holding the fate of everyone at the table. It was up to him to roll a hard eight—two fours. Jax shifted his stance, turned and caught the arm of a cocktail waitress, stalling her in her tracks. The deepest shade of emerald green eyes he'd ever seen stared at him. She was much shorter than he and wore her blond hair in a braid down her back. For a split second, he felt a connection, a spark, a sizzle in the air between them. Jax smiled, holding the dice out to her. An unusual chill skittered across his open palm as if a burst of air-conditioning touched only that spot and nothing else. He held her gaze with his, lost for a moment in her presence, before he found his voice.

"Would you mind blowing on these for luck?"

Her eyebrow hitched as she studied him, while balancing a tray in her other hand. He wasn't sure if he saw amusement or annoyance in her stare. He was surprised when she complied and gently blew on the dice. "Here's to luck."

Jax released her arm, turned and tossed the dice. The table erupted in cheers when they bounced around, landing with two fours upright, creating the needed hard eight. His buddies slapped his back and high-fived excitedly. He couldn't believe they'd just won. While everyone was celebrating, he turned to thank the pretty waitress. The spot where she'd stood was empty. He frantically searched the sea of patrons, craning his neck and lifting to his toes, looking for the woman. Sadly, she was gone, but not forgotten.

Chapter Two

"I've got to find her," Jax proclaimed, tossing hundred-dollar chips for their tips to each of the dealers, the boxman and the stickman. He turned to Arnie and Dennis. "Let's cash out. I'm going to look for her."

"Who?" Dennis asked. "Who are you going to look for?"

"The waitress who blew on the dice for luck. Didn't you see her?"

Dennis shrugged. "No, man. I was too busy eyeing that woman in red at the far end of the table. The way her breasts jiggled when she bounced, I thought for sure they'd pop right out of her top when you rolled that hard eight."

Arnie laughed. "Man, boobs are going to be the death of you."

"What a way to go," Dennis replied with a grin and wag of his eyebrows. "Face planted between a perfect pair, I could suffocate and die a happy man."

"Seriously, neither one of you saw her?" Jax peered into the crowd, searching for his mystery woman.

"Are *you* sure you did?" Arnie teased. "Maybe she was a figment of your imagination." Jax shot him a look that had him changing his tune. "Sorry! We'll help you find her." He turned back to the table, exchanging all the smaller denomination chips for larger ones, making it easier to carry their substantial winnings.

Jax and Dennis each grabbed a handful of their chips, stuffed them in their pockets, then stepped away from the table, leaving Arnie to finish the task. "What did she look like?" Dennis said.

"About this tall," Jax stated with his hand held to where he estimated the top of her head had been. "She wore her hair in a long braid down her back. She's blond and had on that sparkly, silver tank top the cocktail waitresses wear, and she was carrying a drink tray." He snapped his fingers as a thought hit him. "The tray was loaded with used glasses. Bet she was headed to the kitchen to drop them off."

At the same time Arnie turned to join them, the pit boss approached them. "Good evening, gentlemen. Congratulations on your win."

"Thank you," Arnie replied. "Your craps table has been most generous."

"Are you staying here at the Excelsior?"

"Yes, we checked in this morning," Jax answered. He was feeling impatient, not wanting to waste another minute not looking for the blonde. "If you'd excuse us, we were just about to try something else for a while." He lied, hoping the pit boss would let them pass.

"Good evening, gentlemen." The three turned in unison to see a petite brunette approach them, and it hit him. This was the reason the pit boss had stalled them. He'd seen enough shows and movies set in Vegas to know the casinos battled to keep their high rollers playing at their tables. She had stunning big brown eyes, was impeccably dressed in a dark blue, silky sheath dress with matching stilettos. She held her hand out to Jax in a formal greeting. "I'm Veronica and I'll be your host for the rest of your stay. On behalf of the Excelsior, we'd like to move you into a complimentary suite."

Arnie stepped forward, taking her hand and tucking it into the crook of his arm, as he led her away from the table. "Well now, Veronica, tell us more about this suite." He nodded at Jax. "Dennis and I can handle this. We'll text you our new room number. You go find that girl."

Jax didn't hesitate. He weaved his way through the crowd and rows of gaming tables and slot machines. Frustration ate at him, until another cocktail waitress brushed past him with a full tray. He followed her. There had to be a central location where they were returning the dirty glasses. As the one woman pushed the swinging doors to enter the kitchen, another came out with an empty tray.

The blonde! Jax did his best to approach her casually, but it didn't go as planned in his head. She wasn't looking as she turned into him, tripped, and would have fallen if he hadn't caught her. When their gazes met, he held on to her longer than he should have, but she didn't seem to mind. He liked the feel of her in his arms.

"Hi," he managed to say. "I've been looking for you, to thank you."

"Thank me?" she asked, gaining her balance and stepping out of his embrace.

"Yes. You blew on the dice and I won."

She smiled as she shook her head. "I highly doubt it had anything to do with me. I'm not exactly the picture of luck."

"You are to me," he replied, then realized how corny that must've sounded. "I'd like to repay you. Have dinner with me, tonight, please?"

The blush that colored her cheeks made her that much more appealing to him. For a second, he thought she'd say yes. In an instant, her mood darkened. Her eyes widened and she stammered, "I can't, but thank you for asking."

She hurried away, getting lost in the sea of people before he could stop her. Jax looked over his shoulder, sensing someone behind him, but all he saw was the swing of the kitchen door. His phone vibrated. He read the text message.

Meet us on the top floor, the Sunrise Suite. It's got three bedrooms and the best view of the strip.

Chapter Three

Jax sat with his back to the corner. Their casino host, Veronica, had scored them reservations at one of the hottest restaurants in town, *LaGasse's*. The view over his right shoulder was remarkable. Bright lights of Vegas flashed and danced, illuminating the Strip for a mile or so in either direction. Across from him sat Arnie and Dennis both perusing the menu and sipping from their drinks. The Maîtred' had seated them at a table where Veronica had champagne waiting for them.

"Well, guys," Arnie stated, lifting his glass in a toast. "To the experience of a lifetime. Who would've thought coming here on a whim would've turned out so prosperous?"

"Let's not let it go to our heads, and remember where we came from," Dennis added, raising his glass. "Humble beginnings, strong work ethics and a solid drive to achieve our goals in the gaming industry."

"No worries, here," Jax said. "Winning at craps was a fluke. We came to have fun and relax. Nothing more." He eyed his two best buds. "I say we roll our winnings into the company and treat our employees to a bonus and a big-ass party when we return."

"I like that idea," Arnie agreed.

"I second it." Dennis nodded, as they touched their glasses solidifying the toast. "But I don't see why we can't take in a bit of the entertainment while we're here."

Jax turned his head following Dennis' line-of-sight. Veronica strolled through the restaurant directly to their table.

"I see you gentlemen seem to be settled in okay."

"Yes, thanks to you." Dennis smiled. The chemistry between the two was almost palpable in the air.

As Dennis and Arnie discussed the shows available with Veronica, Jax sipped quietly from his drink and studied his menu. There was one woman who lingered in his thoughts. The blonde. He couldn't get her off his mind. They'd wandered through the gaming floor several times before showering, changing and heading to dinner. But he hadn't found her.

When Veronica cleared her throat, Jax realized their table had gone silent. He lifted his eyes from the menu and met Veronica's smiling face. "I'd like you to meet your server for this evening. Jody."

She stepped sideways toward Dennis, revealing a woman dressed in a white button-down shirt with a black bow tie, black slacks and a matching half-apron. But it was her emerald green eyes that caught and held Jax's attention.

Veronica nodded toward Dennis. "If you'll excuse me, I'll go and check on those show tickets you asked about."

Jax stood, extending his hand to Jody. Those brilliant greens of hers widened with recognition. "I'm Jax. I didn't get the chance to properly introduce myself, earlier," he stammered, waving a hand toward his friends. "We want to thank you. I really believe we won because you blew on the dice and gave us luck."

"No, it was just a coincidence." She shook her head, giving him a polite, yet weak smile.

"I don't believe in coincidences," he said softly. She seemed to squirm, not liking the attention he was giving her, so he sat, hoping to make her more comfortable without him looming over her. At six-foot-two, he was tall compared to most, but beside her petite frame, he felt like a giant.

He noted Jody's hand trembled as she resumed her role as their server. Though he tried not to stare, he couldn't help it. Something about her drew him to her. He listened intently as she rattled off the specials for the evening. She patiently answered each of his questions except for one he slipped in at the end of his order.

"Will you have drinks with me later?" He stared directly in her eyes and read interest mixed with nervousness. Damn. He'd never met a woman this skittish in his whole dating life.

She froze. For a second, he thought she might say yes, but the words, "No, thank you," exited on a whisper. It was as if she couldn't move fast enough, weaving through the tables toward the kitchen. What the hell had he said? Jax sat back watching her braid bob along her back as she retreated. This wasn't over. Not by a long shot.

*

Jody whispered in a demanding tone as she passed Veronica at the bar. "Kitchen. Now."

It seemed like an eternity as she waited for her near the huge walk-in freezer at the back of the kitchen. She paced trying to decide how to handle this without losing her temper and her job. Her cousin, Veronica was a silent partner with Derrick LaGasse who had opened *LaGasse's* a year ago. Jody had no doubt Veronica was behind her being hired as a waitress. She needed this second job. Jody wrung her hands. The one person who'd loved her and been her rock for most of her life now depended on her. The Sunnyside Assisted Living facility wasn't cheap. When she was young, she could've ended up in child services after her parents died in a tragic car accident, but her maternal grandma had taken custody of her and raised her. Jody closed her eyes as she pinched the bridge of her nose, trying to stave off the impending headache. After the last time the police found her elderly grandmother wandering down the middle of the road, Jody came to terms with an ominous fact. She couldn't take care of a victim of Alzheimer's. The click of high heels on the tile floor snapped her out of her thoughts and Jody spun to face Veronica.

"Jody, what's the matter?"

"Don't take that innocent tone with me." Jody shook her finger at Veronica as she tried to keep her voice down and her anger in check. There was no need to cause a scene in front of any of the other employees working in the kitchen. "You know exactly what's wrong. I never should've told you some cute guy asked me to blow on his dice."

"Honey, his friends told me about it before you did," Veronica practically purred. "When they described the woman he was looking for, I knew exactly who it was even before you confirmed it."

"*What?*"

"You made quite the impression. He wanted to meet the woman who gave him a breath of luck. I think he's interested in more than that." Veronica nodded toward the restaurant. "If you ask me, he's not bad looking. His dice wouldn't be the only thing I'd blow on."

"Ugh. Veronica, you're hopeless." Jody crossed her arms over her chest. "I can't wait on his table. I'll have to trade off."

"Oh, no, you don't. I got you assigned to that table." Veronica arched an eyebrow and put her hands on her hips. Jody hated it when she took that superior boss attitude. "I take my job over at the Excelsior very seriously. It's how I made the money to buy into this place. You know how competitive I am and that I love being their most successful casino host. *He's* my newest client, a big winner, and we're going to treat him like one. He wanted to meet you and as his host, I made it happen."

"He asked me to meet him for drinks."

"Then your shift ends when they are done dining." Veronica smiled, relaxing her stance. "It's just drinks. I'm not asking you to sleep with him."

"Yeah, I'm not like you. One-nighters aren't my thing," Jody stated bluntly then regretted the words ten seconds after they'd spewed from her lips. "I'm sorry. I didn't mean..."

"Oh, honey. I know you didn't mean it. No harm done. Not everyone can be as fabulous as me," Veronica teased, tilting her chin and sweeping her hands down her toned, petite frame.

Jody shook her head, grateful her cousin was as flamboyantly beautiful and self-confident as she was—the total opposite of herself, the work-alcoholic homebody, though not by choice but out of necessity. But if she had a choice...

"You know I can't be seen with him. What if Carlos finds out?" Jody practically pleaded.

Veronica stood directly in front of her, cutting off any possibility of her leaving. "You deserve to have some fun. You work way too hard. I know you do it to pay for your grandmother's care. Besides, Carlos doesn't own you. You've never even dated. Don't let him scare you into not living your life. They never proved Carlos did it."

"I know he did it. You know he did it. Everyone knows he did it, but his uncle... " Jody shook her head. "Henry would still be alive if it wasn't for his friendship with me. I can't meet with this guy. I can't risk it."

"You listen to me right now." Veronica caught her by the elbows and made Jody look at her. "Henry wouldn't want you living in fear. He didn't. He was your best friend. Respect his memory by living a little." She pulled Jody into a hug. "Maybe you're wrong. Maybe it was just a wrong place, wrong time thing and Carlos didn't kill him."

"I know he did it. He's crazy."

"I agree. Carlos is nuts but he has no hold on you as long as you don't let him." Veronica leaned back, looking her in the eyes. "You're a beautiful soul who needs a life. I won't let you hide in the shadows any longer because of that asshole. Grandmama wouldn't want this either. She'd have your ass if she knew you were letting some jerk scare you. So you might as well accept it." She grinned big. "You've got a date tonight."

Veronica saying the name everyone close to her had called her grandmother—Grandmama, touched a soft spot deep inside her. She and Veronica were cousins because their fathers were brothers. Her maternal grandmother had been a giving soul, spewing wisdom and love on everyone who entered her home. Being the same age, she and Veronica had bonded in their early years and had spent many a sleepover in her grandmother's home. Jody sighed, relinquishing the useless fight. She knew there was no winning against Veronica. Secretly, she accepted the fact she wanted Jax.

"I don't have anything to wear," Jody said weakly, knowing Veronica had an answer for that one even before she said it.

"Swing by my office. You can pick something from the stash of clothes I keep there."

Chapter Four

Her insides quaked as she stood in the doorway of the Piano Lounge. She couldn't believe she was doing this. When he'd grabbed her elbow on the gaming floor, she'd almost whacked him with her tray. But his eyes had caught her attention and prevented her from action. Something about him had filled her thoughts since that moment, even though she'd fought it. She closed her eyes, steadying her nerves, and tried to convince herself nothing good could come of this. When she opened them, her focus landed on the object of her desire and nothing else mattered but him.

The man she only knew as Jax sat at the far end of the bar. The light above him put him in the spotlight, shining on his short blond locks and accentuating the blue of his eyes. When he became aware she'd arrived, he smiled, sporting dimples that made him even more gorgeous. A cool sensation pressed to the low of her back, as if nudging her forward. Jody glanced over her shoulder but nothing was there.

He stood and waved. She had no choice. He'd seen her. She couldn't back out now, not without looking like a fool. The one good thing, the Piano Lounge was in a less populated section of the casino, making it more private. *And off Carlos' radar.* She could do this. Veronica was right. She deserved to have a life. She breathed deeply, wishing for just one night of pleasure. He took her hand and guided her to a table in the back corner beside the bar. Before he sat, he signaled the bartender, who handed him an open bottle of red wine and two glasses. Jax poured them each a glass.

"I hope you like red. This is my favorite Chianti."

"I do." She took a nervous sip. "This is delicious. Thank you."

"I have to tell you." He stared directly at her. "I was surprised to get that note from you about meeting here."

"It's my way of saying thank you too. That was a rather large tip you left me." It was enough to cover her grandmother's medication for a week. At first, she had been torn between giving it back to him as being too much or just keeping it to help with the bills. Veronica insisted she not embarrass her client by trying to return it. Jody nervously swirled the wine in her glass. His next words soothed her indecision, yet almost spurned a discussion on the validity of luck. She'd lived here all her life and had seen way too many people lose everything based on their belief in luck. Good and bad.

"It was the least I could do for you sharing your luck with us." He stopped her protest before she could speak by lifting his glass. "Here's to spending time in one another's company and getting to know each other, whether you believe in luck or not."

They each took a sip, then he extended his hand to her across the table. "My name is Jaxton Cooper, but everyone calls me Jax. I'm from Scarsdale, New York and I'm here to relax and enjoy the sights. One of which is very beautiful and sitting across from me."

Heat filled her cheeks. No one had ever said something so nice to her before. She swallowed against the lump in her throat. "I'm Jody Jorgenson and I'm a born and bred Vegas gal."

As their hands lingered, hovered over the table, the player piano began to play a slow dance number. There was one other couple in the place, who stood and moved to the dance floor.

"May I have this dance?"

For some reason, she couldn't deny him. "Yes."

He guided them around the floor in a slow, graceful rhythm of steps and spins that impressed her. They laughed, talked and danced, getting to know one another. One song flowed into the next until many songs later the music stopped. Breathless, she stood in his arms. The moment was magical. *Kiss him,* whispered through her thoughts. His lips touched hers, hesitant at first then grew bolder as each relaxed into the other.

The lights flashed off and on, snapping them from their kiss. The bartender called out, "Last call. We close in ten."

His forehead pressed to hers. His hand cupped the back of her head as they lingered on the quiet dance floor. His warm breath feathered across her lips and he spoke, "I don't want this to end. Come upstairs with me?"

For the life of her, she couldn't say no. She couldn't speak. A soft voice seemed to whisper in her ear: *take a chance, life's too short not to.* She simply nodded. He took her hand and led her to the elevators.

"Did I hear that old player piano?" the busboy cleaning the tables asked the bartender.

"Yep."

"Didn't know they got it fixed."

"I didn't know it either. Damn thing just started." The bartender shrugged, closing the cover on the dusty old keyboards. "Odd, this

109

hasn't been opened in years."

Chapter Five

"You're in the Sunrise Suite?" Her voice held a hint of awe in its tone.

"Is that something special?" he asked, ushering her inside and closing the door behind them.

Jody wandered around the sitting area. "This suite is haunted."

"You believe in ghosts, but not luck?" Jax couldn't help but smile. He'd never given much thought to the idea of ghosts being real.

"Not sure. I've never seen one." She sat on the arm of the large white sofa. Jax liked the way her eyes shone as she told the tale. "In the sixties, this suite belonged to Luigi 'Lucky' DiBonadetta, the right-hand man of Louis 'The Lip' LaFica, who was the original owner of the Excelsior. Lucky fell in love with a singer named Lolita Constantine. The story goes that Lucky's ex-wife wanted him back. She shot them both, killing Lolita almost instantly. Lucky put a bullet in his ex's head, before he died placing an engagement ring in Lolita's hand. It happened in this very suite."

Jax took her in his arms, tugging her from the couch. "Romantic in a bloody-triple-homicide sort of way."

"You could say that," she said wryly.

Jody's hands were flat against his chest as if ready to push away at any moment. Jax snaked his hand in between them, taking one of hers in his. "This only goes as far as you want, no more."

Kiss her, whispered on a chill close to his ear, causing him to glance sideways for a second then back to Jody, certain he imagined it.

Kiss him, brushed her ear, as if spoken from a woman's lips, but no one was there. Jody shivered. Had she heard the suggestion or simply thought it because she wanted it. Jody stretched as he lowered, meeting her mouth in a gentle kiss. She leaned back, staring up at him. "I want this."

Jax lifted her and carried her into his bedroom, shoving the door closed with his foot. Slowly, she slid down his body and stood on shaky legs at the foot of the bed. Holding his gaze with hers, she unbuttoned the two pearl buttons at the back of her neck, lowering the dresses halter-top. Nerves toyed with her confidence until Jax's fingers trailed along her arm then brushed a perky nipple.

111

"Beautiful," he stated huskily.

Jody shimmied out of the dress, letting it pool around her feet. She wore only a lacy black thong and the high heels. Jax removed his tie as she undid his shirt buttons. Lean muscles graced her palm as she slid her hands inside and pushed the shirt off his shoulders. He shrugged it from his arms. Jody sat on the bed. Jax hurriedly stripped his shoes, socks and pants, leaving his boxers. He caged Jody in between his arms as he leaned into her, kissing her passionately, sending a thrill from her head to her toes. She wanted this more than even she had realized.

Jax left a trail of kisses from her lips, to her jaw, along her neck to the vee between her breasts. He nuzzled from one to the other, as he sucked and teased each nipple, breathing heatedly against her flesh. "Perfect. Jody, you're so beautiful."

Slowly he lowered to his knees. "Lie back. Let me love you."

When he tugged her hips to the edge, she fell backward. He made quick work of her thong, slipping it off and tossing it into the pile with her dress. He took turns kissing along her inner thighs, removing her shoes when he reached each foot. Slowly, he worked his way upward, until his hot lips nuzzled her soft, feminine folds. A leisurely lick made her squirm as he tasted her, tenderly at first, then his tongue's flicking of her clit nearly caused her to implode. She fisted the comforter, pumping her hips in rhythm with his masterful ministrations, until she could hold out no longer.

"Jax," she gasped.

"Come for me, baby," he murmured. He plunged two fingers into her and it was the extra shove she needed to ride the orgasm wave.

Jody lay there breathing heavily, legs wide open as he kissed his way back up her body. Their mouths met in a delicious kiss. He nipped her ear as he guided her farther onto the bed until they reached the pillows. Jax pulled the covers down, ushering her into a comfortable position. He grabbed his pants and obtained a condom from his wallet.

She cocked an eyebrow and smiled. "I love a prepared man."

He stepped out of his boxers. Jody enjoyed the sight of him as he rolled the condom on, then eased onto the bed beside her. His voice was raspy and sexy. "Last chance to back out of this."

"Not a chance in hell." She clasped him behind the neck, pulling him closer as she kissed him.

Jax eased into her.

"Oh, God," she moaned.

He froze. "You okay?" He pressed his brow to hers. Concern filled his tone.

She nodded. "Yeah. It's just been a long time since I've... " Her voice trailed, and she knew her cheeks were flushed.

Jax kissed her nose and grinned. "It's been a while for me too. Hope I haven't forgotten how to do this."

Jody shook her head as the smile broke her lips. "Umm. No. You've done everything right."

"So have you." He rocked slowly and the sensation made her shiver.

Being with Jax was phenomenal. He filled her, teased her, brought her to the edge then held off, starting the dance all over again and again until neither could resist the temptation any further. He pounded into her. Jody dug her heels into the bed, meeting him thrust for thrust. She clung to him as the orgasm erupted, taking them both into the abyss of satisfaction.

Sweat-soaked bodies held each other, touching and kissing tenderly until Jax had no choice but to get up to discard the condom. When he returned, they snuggled, talking until the sunrise.

"I should go," she stated on a whisper.

Jax's arm tightened around her. "Stay. Let's take a nap then do this all over again."

"Umm," she groaned. "I have to be at work by two. I'll stay until noon. That'll give me time to go home and change."

He kissed her, pulling her closer, wrapping his whole body around her. Jody had never felt so safe. Closing her eyes, it was the first time in months that she'd been this happy.

Hours later, she woke to the most wonderfully handsome man she'd ever known, brushing the hair from her eyes.

"Wake up, sleepyhead. It's eleven. I ordered room service. It should be here soon. Thought I'd refurbish your energy before I ravish you in the shower." His dimpled smile brightened her day instantly. The feel of his hard-on rubbing against her leg through the sheet had her ready to play.

Jody cupped his cheek. "Want a good morning quickie?"

"Who could say no to that?" He grinned, capturing her mouth in

113

a kiss and crawling back under the covers with her.

*

"Room service."

The knock on the door brought Jax out of the bathroom wearing an Excelsior bathrobe. The doors to his friends' rooms were closed, so he figured they were asleep. Jody followed behind him dressed in nothing but a robe, and had her hair wrapped in a towel. Sex may have started in the bed, but they'd finished in the shower. Best shower he'd ever experienced. He grinned at her as he opened the door.

It swung inward hard, slamming Jax against the wall and pinning him there. The food cart crashed into the door of one of the other bedrooms. A man lunged toward Jax, fisting the front of the robe and jerking him from behind the door. Before Jax had his footing, the man sucker-punched him.

"Carlos! What the fuck!" Jody screamed.

The dark-haired man released Jax and went after Jody. She ran, placing the couch between them. "You belong to me, Jody. I've told you this before."

She threw a pillow at him, which he swatted away. "We've never even gone out. What the fuck is wrong with you?"

Surprise filled Carlos' face when he was tackled from behind. Jax had recovered from the hit and wasn't afraid to fight back. Carlos bounced off the couch and spun to face Jax. He stood a few inches shorter than Jax, but he was a muscle-bound menace, outweighing Jax by at least fifty pounds. That didn't stop Jax. He readied himself for the attack, fists held up, watching for the next move.

Carlos rushed him. Jax sidestepped, landing a solid blow to Carlos' jaw. Blood spurted, as Carlos wiped it with the back of his hand. He righted himself and sprang at Jax again, this time wrapping him up and shoving him into the wall. Carlos swung wildly, planting a couple of blows to Jax's gut. Jax pushed him back enough that he could get in a decent uppercut that dazed Carlos, who wobbled backward. Jax readied to hit him again, but didn't get the chance. Carlos drew a gun and pointed it at him.

A high-pitched screech filled the air. *"Not again! This will not happen again!"* Instantly, a woman and a man flashed between Carlos

114

and Jax. A rush of energy from the female ghostly figure forced the gun to fly from Carlos' hand, while the man's hands wrapped around his neck. Carlo's eyes widened in fear as a gasp escaped his throat.

Clang! The sound of metal hitting a hard object split the air. Carlos' eyes rolled back in his head and he crumpled to the floor. Jody stood on the coffee table with the solid silver lid from the serving tray in her hand. Jax stepped over the unconscious man and gathered her in his arms as she dropped the lid. She shook from head to toe, pressing her face against his chest for a moment then they turned to look at the pair who'd intervened.

The woman wore a silver gown and the man was dressed in an old-fashioned suit. The transparent figures smiled. *"We couldn't let it happen again."* The woman reached as if to stroke Jody's cheek. *"Waste no time, for it is short. Love and be loved. Take the chance."*

The pair disappeared.

Jody looked up at Jax. Her voice strained and hardly above a whisper, she asked, "You believe in ghosts now?"

"Without a doubt." He brushed a kiss to her brow.

"Is he dead?" He heard the hitch in her voice and knew she was scared.

"No," he reassured her, tilting her chin to meet her gaze. Tears hovered on the verge of falling. "Who is he?"

"I'll tell you who he is." Both of them turned at the sound of a woman's voice.

Veronica came out of Dennis' room, tying a robe closed around her. Dennis was right behind her, pulling on a pair of sweats. "He's a no-good, lying asshole, who's been stalking my cousin, Jody. That's who he is." She snatched up the room phone and issued orders into it. "Get security and the police to the Sunrise Suite, *immediately.*"

Arnie walked in the open door, carrying a cardboard tray filled with coffee cups. His eyes widened. "What the hell did I miss?"

Jax looked at him over the top of Jody's head while he continued to console her. "A fight. This guy came here trying to claim someone who didn't belong to him."

"Looks like he crossed the wrong guy," Dennis said, kneeling beside Carlos' unconscious body, checking him for a pulse.

"I need to sit down," Jody gasped, visibly trembling.

Jax helped Jody to the couch and sat beside her.

Four huge security guards showed up along with the hotel

manager, Edward Menendez. He shook his head, staring down at his unconscious nephew. Veronica got in his face.

"He fucked up this time, Edward. There's a room full of witnesses. Can't sweep this under the rug now, can you?"

Jody pointed to the gun lying underneath the coffee table. "I bet that's the missing gun used to kill Henry."

"Who's Henry?" Jax asked.

"He was my best friend and he was murdered," Jody answered on a whisper.

When Edward started toward the gun, Dennis stood in his way. "Not sure what's going on here, but you're not touching that."

"I wouldn't if I were you," Arnie piped in, holding his cell phone for all to see. He spun around snapping pictures. With a press of his thumb, he stated smugly, "Just sent those safely to two virtual storage locations. Wouldn't want any sort of evidence to go missing, in case it's important."

Veronica flopped onto the couch beside Jody, placing an arm around her, while her gaze remained directly on Edward. "Is that fear in your eyes, Edward? I sense Jody's right. Your crazy-ass nephew killed her friend, Henry, because he thought they were dating. Hate to tell you this, but Henry was gay. Jody has never had any interest in Carlos. She's told him that multiple times. I wouldn't doubt you're the reason she can't get a restraining order against him. Just how deep do your paws go?"

Edward stepped back. "I assure you, I had nothing to do with any of it." He turned, straightening his coat, and walked toward the door.

One of the security guards caught his arm. "What do you want us to do with him?"

"Let the cops have him." Edward shrugged, indignantly. "I'm done with him."

When the cops arrived, Carlos was arrested. Everyone gave their statements as to what they knew, but Jody and Jax left out the most important part. The appearance of Lucky and Lolita was a secret they planned to keep.

Late that night after everyone was in bed, Lolita stood beside Lucky on the balcony outside the Sunrise Suite. She laid her head on his shoulder. "That was a good thing we did. They make a perfect couple."

Lucky put his arm around her waist. "I'm glad you spotted them in the casino. If you hadn't guided her toward that table, they never would've met."

She nudged his side. "You're the one who made her breath a lucky one, making those dice land on an eight. You sly devil."

"You're the one who gave her a shove when she almost chickened out at the lounge." He cupped her chin.

"But it was your playing that made them fall in love." She turned in his arms. "That's how you won me. When you played the piano, I always sang my best. Your fingers were magical on the keyboard."

He wagged his eyebrows as he leaned closer for a kiss. "Come here and let me show you what else is magical on me."

The pair faded away locked in an eternal embrace.

Six months later

Jody stood on the front porch of their new home. She still couldn't believe she'd left Vegas for Scarsdale, but she was so glad she did. The long distance love affair hadn't dwindled like she'd been afraid that it would. Instead, it'd blossomed into a lifelong commitment. She'd met the perfect man. He'd even helped relocate her grandmother to a facility dedicated to the care of Alzheimer's patients that was one town over from them. Close enough she could visit every day.

She wiggled her finger as she watched the sunlight twinkle off the two-carat, oval diamond ring and matching platinum wedding band. Breathing in deeply, the scent of cool crisp air filled her nose. A set of warm arms encircled her waist, tugging her against him.

"Having second thoughts?"

She turned in his embrace. "Never. Do you believe in love at first sight?"

"You know that I do. Asking you to blow on those dice was the luckiest thing I ever did in my life. Convincing you to marry me was the smartest."

"You think we'll ever see them again?"

"Lucky and Lolita?"

"Yes."

"Maybe, maybe not, but let's make it a tradition to spend the anniversary of the day we met in Vegas, at the Excelsior in the Sunrise Suite."

"Such the romantic. I love that idea." Jody stretched onto her toes, kissing the love of her life.

7

LOST VEGAS

Ed DeAngelis

Three generations ago, the world fell. Humanity, as many knew it, was wiped clean. There were wars that led up to it, but few now remember what caused them, what caused the people of the world in their final days to rain nuclear death and deadly viruses upon their own kinsman. But humanity did not die—it just changed. Many died, but humanity survived, the will to live stronger than any bomb or any virus. Many were changed. The viruses that killed, now mutated by the massive radiation, altered things: people, animals, plants. Many grew stronger, more dangerous. Those who were left banded together, some to bring light to our ruined world and rebuild, and some to keep it in darkness, keep it torn down for their own desires. As for me? I am just a simple guy trying to survive in this world of darkness.

My gaze wandered over the ruined skyline of what was once Las Vegas. I had been told when I was young, by my grandfather, that this city had been one of the few havens in this once great land before the war. The mountains had protected the city from the worst of the radiation and slowed the spread of infection from the viruses. Thanks to a place he called the Hoov-uh Dam, the power stayed on. But in the end, those things considered blessings and luxuries had become the city's downfall; blessings had become curses as people swarmed from all over, seeking shelter. The city burned from the inside out as people fought for those limited resources. But that was many, many years ago. The city is now a collection of colossal, skeletal wrecks, a memoriam to an age of splendor now long past.

I live in one of those skeletal wrecks, one that was once called the Excelsior.

I crouched behind a few feet of wall, gazing out from what used to be a window, tattered curtains concealing my location from all but the most perceptive of eyes. I spent most of my days here, high up in my small, hidden spot, watching the city. It was boring... most days. But it needed to be done. Empty buildings tended to draw all sorts of foul creatures from the surrounding wastes, and this was my home now. Had been ever since the tribe that had been living here two years past had waged war upon the needle-building tribe and taken it over. They had deemed the Excelsior worthless. I knew better.

The day was a cool one, which I was grateful for. The summers here were terrible and I was glad the days were cooling, although that meant the things that hunted at night were coming out earlier. The goggles I wore shielded my eyes as a blast of sand-filled wind gusted past me into the now, mostly empty room. Upon the howl of the wind I heard others—rad coyotes. Hefting my trusty but beaten hunting rifle, I pressed my goggle-protected eye to the end of the scope, using it in an attempt to locate them. Movement flashed across my line of sight, and I yanked the scope away, eyes locking on the area I had been scanning. A cloaked figure darted around debris and along piles of sand. The slender figure ran for its life, as behind it came four scrawny, mangy creatures, their sleek bodies mostly hairless and covered in glowing green sores, slavering jaws wide as they bounded after their prey. Their prey was not helpless, as I saw the person gripping what looked like a bow. My assumption was correct, for upon the stranger's back I noticed a nearly empty quiver.

One of the coyotes leapt ahead of the rest, its hunger and madness brought on by the radiation mutations driving it to almost impossible speeds. I jerked my rifle up but found that action unneeded, as the beast lunged for the figure, propelling itself off the ruined shell of a vehicle. The figure spun, cloak swirling around it making the person almost a blur. From that blurring swirling figure, an arrow flew. Lancing into the lunging beast, it sank within the confines of the creature's skull. The coyote fell without sound, without struggle. And that blurred figure, without missing a step, continued his mad dash toward the closest shelter: the Excelsior.

My thoughts rattled around in my head in a hundred different directions, each one moving as fast as the stranger running below. It took me a moment to gather them. But when I finally did, I found myself hauling my butt out of the room, slinging my rifle across my back to keep it safe, and booking it down the old, dried-carpeted hallway. I didn't have time for the stairs, so as I rounded the corner, my heart pounding, I lunged for an open doorway, but *this* doorway had no room behind it, only a long black tunnel going down waiting to swallow me. There were long, thick metal cables that my hands grabbed to keep me from falling into the abyss. And like all the tunnels in the Excelsior but one, there was a large box within it, but thankfully, this tunnel's box was higher up. Old, toughened leather gloves grew hot as I slid down the wire, plummeting into the darkness, every few seconds passing a flash of light from another floor. The ground was approaching rapidly, and my hands tightened. The smell of burnt leather filled my nostrils and my descent began to slow. The muscles in my arms and shoulders screamed in protest, but I had done this before, though normally much more slowly, and by using my legs to shimmy down. But time was of the essence and I trusted my body to not give out on me. The person below was relying on me.

With a resounding thud, my worn boots slammed into a pile of old mattresses, sending clouds of dust puffing up around them. I had thrown them down here to lessen my impact after my first attempt had left me with a sprained ankle. My body took a moment to recover, as the impact was still jarring. My racing heart pumped adrenaline through my body, helping me, for at least the moment, to ignore any of the lesser pain I would feel. I scrambled up and over the small ledge between the mattress-covered floor and the doorway to the main lobby. There was still time. I could hear the rattling and bashing as the person tried to open the many doors. But I had sealed them all. The only way into this building was to be let in—well, the only non-violent-based way in, as the charred and crackled archway

121

toward one section of the sealed doorways showed. I ran to the door, only to be stopped in my tracks. I heard the stranger's voice for the first time; it was soft, sweet, yet fierce. And unmistakably female.

"If ye want some of me, come and get some, foul mangy beasts!" Her challenge was answered by two snarls and yips—only two—the third she must have taken down.

A woman. My mind reeled at the thought. Quickly, my hands fumbled with the locks that I normally should have been able to flip open in a split second, yet now it was like trying to open a massive safe. Finally, after what seemed like an eternity, the locks clicked and the barricaded door was thrust open. Light streamed in, and silhouetted inside was the cloaked woman. The door startled her and she spun around, her bow now lay lengthwise across her back, the quiver empty, and a long, wicked-looking scrap blade was held in a slender hand. I had only a glimpse of fiery red locks and piercing green eyes before I raised my rifle and focused on the sickly green thing that was surging toward her exposed back. The crack of the rifle echoed through the lobby and out into the street. The slender female dropped to the floor, and an inch behind her, the rad coyote also dropped. Its powerful jaws, filled with razor-sharp teeth still snapped for a few moments, even though death had already claimed it. The other one froze. Most of its pack was gone, and despite the madness and strength the radiation brought, deep within its mind it knew it was outnumbered and that the sound of a gun meant death. It turned tail and ran.

My sense of relief was short-lived, and in a momentary lapse of judgement I allowed my eyes to close, and I exhaled deeply. The cold, hard kiss of steel against my neck snapped my mind back to the moment. And my eyes opened to see the young woman gazing up at me, hard—yet beautiful—eyes gazed into mine, judging, calculating.

"Ye... shot... at me."

I wanted to say something, to tell her to look behind her, but that milky skin, the array of freckles upon her delicate features... Even though her voice had warmth, I knew the tone was deadly. It enchanted and befuddled my mind. She was *beautiful*. It was not like I had not seen females before, just none had looked like this one: a slender, pale-skinned angel with fiery, curly locks. The sharp edge of the knife slid slightly in her hand, and the sting of its kiss finally loosened my tongue.

"No, no, not you. The rad coyote behind you." I attempted to point, but the moment my arm began to move, I felt more pressure from the knife.

Her hooded head turned slightly, one eye still locked on me, watching for deceit. Her eyes flicked toward the dead rad coyote, which was still twitching, then back to me. Slowly, I felt the cold knife-edge pull away, and with a rapid flourish, she sheathed the blade. She spun around. Her green patchwork cloak swirled around her as she stalked back outside. Coming back after a few moments, her quiver was now restocked. She stopped next to me, where I had remained. My now bare hand rubbed the small cut on my neck. She reached up, pulling my hand away.

"Ye will be fine. Now hurry yer arse up and lock the door, and we can begin the pleasantries."

"I... um... sure." I moved up, closing the door, locking it. My eyes gazed at the surrounding buildings that had a view of the courtyard. *I hope they didn't see her.* With the door closed and locked, I turned, just in time to see that large hood pulled back. A massive, unruly pile of red curls spilled forth, framing a tiny face. A beautiful face: a swirl of fire transformed into hair.

Soft plump lips curved into a smirk as they caught my stare. "What? Have ye never seen a woman before? Stop all the slack-jawed gawking and tell me yer name." She fisted her pale hands and placed them on her tattered jean-covered hips. Head cocking slightly, she met my gaze with her own. Although the fierceness had faded from her eyes, it still glittered within them.

Her accent made my skin tingle and my pulse quicken. I wanted her. I needed her. Never before had a woman so enchanted me. I had just met her, and yet I yearned for her approval, her acceptance, and her desire—but most of all, I wanted—no, I needed—her *love*. But standing here staring at her like some sort of simple-minded yokel would not gain me any of those. I shook my head, clearing my mind. "Of course, I'm sorry, I just don't see many women wandering the city alone. My name is Jack." I extended my hand toward her. "It's is a pleasure to meet you... ?"

Her own slender hand slipped into mine. "Lilandra, but ye can call me Lil."

The softness of that pale, milky flesh made my heart flutter and my stomach roll. I swallowed loudly and shook her hand softly, reluctant to release it, yet forcing myself to. "Lilandra... " The name rolled off my tongue and brought on a whole new wave of butterflies in my gut. "Please follow me. We have a ways to go till we are somewhere safe." I led the way.

We traversed the maze that was the interior of the Excelsior, through a sea of strange rectangle-shaped machines, broken and most lying on their sides. There were hundreds of metal chairs and tables with now faded cloth of some sort that had numbers and other symbols on them. They were everywhere throughout the building. Their purpose was long forgotten, but I had given them a new purpose. They were ponderous things, and I had managed, after many-many attempts, to use them as -simple but effective barricades. Even the ravagers, twisted by the virus and radiation, with their crazed strength, could not force open the doors with these piled behind them. There were scores of things throughout the building, but most of it was just scrap. Many of the things I, and others, would have deemed important had long ago been scavenged by those who had come before me.

Lilandra and I wandered the maze for only a short time until we came upon the small hallway that led to one of the few stairways that led to the upper levels. There were many stairways leading up, but those were liabilities. So over the course of my first year here, I sealed all of them but this one. This one I just filled with massive heaps of rusted metal and broken furniture and all sorts of garbage. It made ascending the stairs a difficult thing, but mainly it was meant to hide the plethora of traps I had concealed within the junk. They were meant to harm and injure a person's legs, making a hard climb even more difficult.

I watched her as she ascended. She was so graceful, her slender legs weaving her around without issue over and in-between any obstacle. Her glance would catch mine from time to time, and a few times mine caught hers. Each glance I caught of those emerald eyes quickened my pulse. Finally, after almost an hour of climbing and carefully bypassing my hidden traps, we made it to the forty-fifth floor. I had chosen this floor because the floors above this had long ago been burned away—the cause unknown. But all that remained above was the skeleton of the building: black, burnt, steel beams reaching skyward. The fire had also caused some structural collapses, sealing off the forty-fifth floor. The others before me must have assumed that that floor was also ruined. When I decided to make this place my home, I'd managed to shift the rock away without causing any further collapse. Once that was accomplished, I had reinforced the doorway and found that the forty-fifth floor was mostly untouched. Many of the windows were still intact, and the rooms, although old and worn from time, were untouched by previous scavengers. And the roof, despite the fire above, was solid enough in most places. Such luxuries were rare and had been a major blessing. And as if untouched rooms weren't amazing enough, I discovered, within a back area, a room stacked ceiling high with a bounty of supplies: crates of canned or dried food, the kind that had been made to last the test of time. Massive jugs of water and various other containers had filled much of the room. The proprietor of my newfound wealth was revealed to me shortly after this discovery while I explored the surrounding rooms. A dusty skeleton greeted me when I entered one of the corner rooms, my current trusty rifle lying across its pelvis. Used cans and empty jugs and bottles of water were scattered around him, as well as all other sorts of supplies. Some of it was still useful, such as the stacks of unused ammo boxes for the rifle. Most of it, though, was worthless. Time ruins all things, just some things slower than others. I took Lilandra there now—well, not to that exact room, but to the one I had claimed.

I watched as Lil paced around my room, exploring the rare luxuries I had within. Walking first toward my bed, she dragged her fingertips slowly across it before making her way over to an intact couch piled with pillows to cover the cracked, leather cushions. The entire one side of the room was one massive window. Tiny cracks covered it, but it was thick and so far had held. Large curtains flanked it. I had them open for now, allowing the setting sun to shine inside. Next to the window, on a raised area of the floor, was the object that drew the most curiosity from Lilandra.

"Why do ye have a plastic, hole-filled pot in the floor?" She turned, her red brows knitted in confusion.

"Let me show you!" The exuberance in my voice must have surprised her, as that knitted brow now rose while I quickly made my way over. The Excelsior still had many secrets that those before me had missed. I had not, and I was eager to impress Lilandra. I squatted down and began to fiddle with knobs and buttons. Below me, the plastic-lined hole began to rattle and shake until the whole floor thrummed. Suddenly water began to shoot from the holes, and rapidly the plastic hole began to fill with odd-smelling, but clear-ish, water.

"Water!" Lil lunged down, pale hands reaching down to scoop at the liquid.

"No!" I lunged for her and pushed her hands away.

She spun around, her eyes wide as she looked at me. "Are ye daft man? I am your guest and am thirsty, yet you smack the water from me hands?"

"That water is not meant for drinking... It's special water, smell it." I nodded toward the clear liquid and watched as she leaned down, her nose twitching as she breathed in deeply before it scrunched up and she jerked back a little.

"'Tis poison!" She scooted back away from the filling hole.

I moved to her, and seeing a chance, I placed my hands on her shoulders. I felt her tense for a moment, but it passed, and to my delight she did not pull away. "It's special water. It's for cleaning yourself, not drinking. And watch. If you give it time, it gets hot. I could see the skepticism in her eyes, but that -soon switched to disbelief, when after a few minutes, once the hole had filled, I had her feel the water once more.

"I'll be damned, it's warm!"

"Give it a little longer and it will get hot, not enough to burn, but hot enough to feel amazing." As I spoke, I handed her one of my canteens filled with water, watching as she greedily gulped it down.

"Ah, much better. Thank ye." She flashed me that brilliant smile of hers before she continued her exploration. She approached the side of my bed, fingers tracing the small switches placed within the wall.

"I wouldn't—" Too late. She pushed down on one, and with a buzz and flicker, the light next to my bed turned on. She gasped and jerked back in surprise, eyes wide as they beheld a room illuminated by artificial light. Just as quick as the light had filled the room, my hand snapped forward and hit the switch, and the light vanished. "Gimme a moment." I smiled at her and made my way to the large window-wall and drew the heavy thick curtains shut. Once closed, I took chairs and other items to push the curtain to the wall along the sides and bottom, sealing it as best I could. Once satisfied, I turned and nodded toward Lil. "Go ahead." I walked back over just in time to watch her hand flick on the light.

"How?" she asked in a stunned, awe-filled voice, looking at the small bulb, back at me, then around the room. "I don't see any batteries. Where does the power come from?"

"This building has many secrets. Some of them were well hidden in halls of stone under the earth. Another was pipes that somehow still carry power. I found one of them and was able route it into the building." I laughed softly as the memories of those days filled my thoughts for a second. "It caused a lot of problems at first, a lot of fires and burns. But eventually I was able make it so the power only went to the places I wanted it to go to. But please, be careful. Others who live in this city think this is a worthless wreck of a building. If they were to find out what things are hidden in here, they would come and take the building and force me to show them how it works, and where things..."

A slender, warm finger pressed to my lips, my warning silenced by the softest of touches. "Shh, no need to be getting yourself into a fit." I plan to be leaving tomorrow. Me family is waiting for me to return. They be waiting on the outskirts of town. I was scouting the city for them, for a path through or around the city. We normally head to the coast through the northern passes, but the ravager tribes up north have been growing and it is too dangerous. So me dad told us there used to be a way through the mountains. We found it then came upon your city. They sent me to scout ahead and seek passage through while the others check for a way around." Her finger slowly slipped from my lips, the warmth of her smile radiated upon my skin, warming my flesh with its radiance. "But until the morning comes to take me away, in your company I will stay."

Her hips swayed softly as she made her way toward the now steaming, water-filled plastic pot. As she sauntered, bits of clothing fell from her like leaves from a tree, littering the ground, revealing patches of pale, unmarred porcelain skin." So this water be for bathing you say?" Her head turned, peering over that smooth shoulder; her eyes twinkled with another kind of fierceness, and her enchanting smile now became inviting. "Well, then, shall we bathe?"

My mouth hung agape, and I felt a tightness in my chest. My brain was a jumble of thoughts. *Leaving? No, you can't leave, you just came here.* My heart shuddered with pain I had never felt nor imagined I could feel. I had to do something, had to convince her to stay.

Somehow I would make her mine. But how?

"Are ye, just gonna stand there all slack-jawed, or will ye join me to... *bathe.*"

The words of invite that passed her supple lips fell sweetly upon my ears like honey upon the tongue. And my worries, for the moment, abated. There would be enough time later to figure out what to do, how to convince her to stay with me. Right now, the desire I had for her was being reciprocated. My eyes focused in time to see her pale, perky breasts dip below the churning, steaming waterline. And the tightness in my chest moved to a more appropriate area. Although my heart now danced to the unsung rhythm of my desires, of my need for her. As I approached Lilandra, I began to strip off my worn, tattered clothes. My green jacket dropped, followed by my tan shirt, covered in countless stitches to patch the various tears and holes that had formed. My years of living here had hardened my body. It was not flawless like hers. My flesh was darker, kissed by many hours in the sun, and covered in scars earned from a hard life. My body was toned from my years of hard labor, but I was not some massive, statuesque man. Lilandra's beautiful eyes shone with approval. I swallowed as my hands went to undo the large buckle I wore on my belt. It was stamped with three letters: NFR. I had no idea what they meant, but it was a good solid belt. I was shaking as excitement filled my body. We would become one tonight. I was sure of it.

The Excelsior suddenly shuddered, like an animal that had been shot. Twice more the building shook. I knew what was happening, even though I couldn't see it. The Excelsior was being besieged.

*

My body froze, as did my heart. *Oh please God not now, not now!* I ran past Lilandra, the confusion and a hint of worry evident on her face. The thick curtains were yanked apart, and my gaze fell to the courtyard below, hundreds of feet down. The many wisps of rising smoke were the first thing my eyes took in, followed by the mob of people who held the torches that produced that smoke. What made the scene worse was the mass of them that were already streaming through the smoking hole that had once been two of three barricaded doors. I wondered for a moment who they were, but that question was answered when I saw a man upon a litter. He stood on the litter, which was being held aloft by four massive brutes, each one chained with a leather mask covering his head. He himself was wearing a long leather duster, although his gut was too massive to be hidden behind it, and a crown of plants adorned his head. He howled orders and pointed a meaty finger at the Excelsior. It was the Palace, and their leader Caesar himself had come to lead his tribe. I was too far up to hear him through the glass, but I knew what—no, not what, but who—he wanted. I spun around, only to find Lilandra was not one to sit idly by. She was already dressing. Her face, which had once been alluring, was now focused and hard.

Her eyes met mine as her hips wiggled into her jeans. "What is going on?"

"Shit, shit, *shit*! We gotta go. They must have seen you!" I ran to gather and toss on my own discarded clothing.

"Who are *they*? And why do *they* care about me?" She moved so much faster than me. Already she was dressed and waiting, while I was still fumbling to get my boots on.

"They are from the Palace. And... they collect women." Today was not a good day for my heart: desire, anxiety, disappointment, utter total terror... not a good combination. The breakneck speed at which my heart pounded filled my ears. Lilandra's voice was but a soft whisper that I struggled to hear. I had prepared for an escape situation, but in all my preparations, I had always assumed the only person needing to escape would be me. But now Lilandra was here, and I *had* to keep her safe. I knew in my mind that I had just met her, and trying to save her could cost me my life; but my heart was already hers, and I could no more leave her than I could rip my own heart from my chest. Both situations would lead to my demise. She was precious to me. But the Palace would not stop until they got her, or they were all dead. And their tribe was very large.

A sudden pain lanced up my arms as if they were being latched onto by a pair of vise-grips. The pain locked my focus, which was now on two pale hands gripping my arms and a pair of green eyes inches from mine.

"Calm yerself, Jack, and tell me who they are. What do you mean by collect? "Her breath blew hot across my stubble-covered face. Her hands slowly released their vise-like grip on my arms.

I swallowed and forced my breathing to slow. "They are the

largest tribe here in Vegas. They live in the Palace, the large building with all the columns. It's across the road. They are ruled by a man who calls himself Caesar. Apparently he named himself after some old warlord who used to inhabit that building. They enslave women. I have been to their building before. I have seen the breeding rooms. Women are kept chained up. They are long chains, and the rooms they inhabit are beautiful and luxurious, but they are still chained within, guards watching them night and day. They are toys for the tribe. Their only purpose is to please the men and birth children. Female children are raised from birth to be just like their mothers."

"Slavers!" The word was more of a hiss than actual speech, that once-beautiful smile now a snarl of unbridled hate and disgust. Her green, patchwork cloak spun past me in a blur, and she hastily grabbed up her few remaining items. Small, black leather gloves were yanked onto her slender hands before she hefted her bow. Her grip was so tight I heard the leather groan.

We needed to hurry, but there were a few more things that I needed. Squatting, I reached under the bed, pulling from under it two medium duffle bags. I dragged them over to Lil and opened them, revealing an array of guns. They were strange looking; some of them with round-shape ammo cartridges. I had never seen their likes before, until I found them hidden deep within the bowels of this place.

"Where did ye find all of those?" Guns were powerful things, ammo even more so, and I had just displayed a treasure-trove of them.

"I think that all the buildings used to once be owned by some kind of warrior or warlord, or something. These and many more like them I found in a hidden room behind a secret wall that had broken open during the quake we had last year. Inside were piles and piles of dust-covered guns, and knives, and all sorts of things. But that's not important. What is, is getting you down to that room, because within it are tunnels. These tunnels lead to all different parts of the city. Some of them are collapsed, but I have explored all the ones that were not, and one leads to a small building near the outskirts of town, close to where your family and caravan is and beyond the reach of the Caesar and the Palace." I tossed her a duffle bag.

As it soared toward her, Lilandra shouldered her bow and grabbed the bag just before it hit the ground. She dug through it for a moment, before pulling out a simple pistol. It was worn, but a faded horse design could still be seen stamped on the metal. She popped the clip out, and satisfied that it was loaded, slammed it back into the handle, and proceeded to cock the gun. Searching through the bag once more, she produced two guns like the first. From these, Lilandra only took the clips, of course checking them for bullets as well. "Come on, then, let's be going."

"Right you are." I shouldered my own bag, after having stuffed some other various items inside: water, canned food, etc. It was a ponderous weight upon my shoulder, but nothing about survival was easy. With that done, I frowned, pausing for a moment to glance around my room: the tube of bathing water, the soft bed, all the things I was leaving behind. But then my gaze fell upon Lilandra, the tiny fierce warrioress that had come running into my life just hours before, and I knew I would give all of this up a hundred times over for just a few more moments with her—even if those moments were me fleeing for my life and her for her freedom.

With that thought steeling my fraying nerves, I booked it out of the room, Lilandra right on my heels. We made our way down the hallway and to the stairwell we had come in by. It was the only open one this level; the rest were collapsed. As we made our way down, I could hear the Palace tribe. They were trying to navigate the stairwell, but from the curses and cries I heard, my traps were slowing them— but not enough. They were overwhelming the traps and scrap piles by sheer numbers. And the knowledge that failure in their tribe came with consequence, worse than anything my traps could do, spurred them forward. We had one advantage: we only had to go down one floor. The Palace still had many, many to climb. Quickly, we leapt over the scrap I had scattered, but there were no traps from my floor. I had done that for a case like this, when I needed to make a hasty withdrawal. So with a few leaps and bounds, Lilandra and I rapidly descended into the clear hallway of the forty-fourth floor. From there I led Lilandra to one of the large tubes that contained boxes, which I had assumed had once taken people up and down the building. But no matter how much I tried to connect power to them and make them run, like I had the light and the bathing pot in my room, they had refused to work. But in doing that, I had found that some of them led to the lower areas. As we approached, I stopped and turned. "Ok, so now this is gonna sound strange, but you see the thick wires in the center of this pit?"

She frowned, a fiery eyebrow cocking. "Of course I be seeing it! I ain't blind."

"Good, we're gonna, one at a time, jump on it."

"Are ye daft? The blasted tunnel looks like it goes all the way down to the gates of hell." She was glaring down into the tunnel of seemingly endless darkness, head slightly shaking back and forth as she spoke.

I sighed. "As I was saying, we're gonna jump on it one at a time and shimmy our way down till we can't go down anymore. It leads all the way down to the place where the tunnels are. Now just watch me and do as I do."

I slung my rifle over my shoulder, along with the duffle bag. I gave Lil my best cocky, "trust me," smile, then I jumped. My gloved hands, for the second time today, sought and clenched around the thick, hanging wires, but this time I remembered to wrap my feet around the wire, applying pressure to help my arms and shoulders out. I swayed back and forth for a moment, as the wire shook slightly. Glancing back at Lil, that cocky smile still on my face, I called out, "See, it's not that b—"

Loud echoing pops began to fill the tunnel, and I saw a spark appear below me. I felt something whizz by my cheek, only to clang against something above me.

"Holy hell!" I was being fired upon. The bastards must have stationed people at this tunnel, and when they saw the wires moving they began to shoot upward. Frantically, I leapt for the edge, desperation fueling my already tired muscles.

My foot caught on the wire. And my normally easily leap fell short, my hands just managing to grasp the edge. An inch less, and I would have plummeted to my doom. My legs kicked frantically at the air, trying to find purchase, while the pop and crack of gunfire continued. I flinched as sparks erupted next to my eyes, and a bullet ricocheted off a metal panel by my head. But I felt that tight vise-like grip of Lilandra once more as she latched onto my arms. My gaze found her shimmering green eyes, and I found comfort and strength within them.

"Come on now, don't go dying on me after we just met."

I heard her grunt of exertion as those little legs flexed. Slowly I began to rise. After a moment, I tumbled over the ledge and barreled right into my slender savior. My body ungracefully plowed into hers, and we tumbled to the floor together, my body lying on top of hers. Our eyes locked. I could feel her chest rising and falling in sync with my own. For a single moment, the danger, the bullets, the growing shouts of people coming to kill, steal, and take vanished, and all that was left was us.

I saw her soft, pink lips quiver. My own lowered to comfort them, eyes closing as they did. But Lil was no timid girl and her lips rose to meet mine halfway. I shuddered as a wave of energy surged out of her mouth and through my body. I longed for more, and my mouth pressed forward hungrily. Then her lips suddenly left mine, my body jerking as the energy she had suffused me with was cut off. My eyes fluttered open, head tilting in confusion. I saw her smile up at me, and with a sharp warm laugh, she pushed me off and rolled onto her knees.

"There be plenty of time for that once we make it out of here. Now, come on, lover boy, we have an escape to pull off." The words purred past her pursed lips, and she winked at me. She grabbed the duffle bag she'd dropped when she'd hauled my ass out of the tunnel.

Gunshots, cries of rage, of excitement, all came rushing back as reality once more asserted itself. I struggled to get up. The cold embrace of near death, followed by the hot, searing fire of Lilandra's touch, had left my body with a hodgepodge of feelings. But I needed to get moving. So pushing all of those feelings down, I forced my reluctant legs to stand and continued to lead Lilandra to the next escape tunnel.

But my carefully laid escape plans were foiled, and my hope began dwindling as one tunnel after another we came upon was guarded. I was more cautious after the first and tested each tunnel thereafter. Using my rifle, I would poke and jiggle the wire, and each time I was greeted with gunfire from below.

After we had tested the final tunnel, I began to pace back and forth. I didn't know what to do, and my mind raced. *How could they have known about the tunnels? How could they have known which ones were not blocked by the boxes? What are we going to do? Can't go to the stairs. Maybe some of those blocked— No, no don't be stupid; they're sealed tight. You don't have time. Maybe... shoot the people at the bottom of the tunnels. Wait, no, think, Jack. Think! You can't see them, and they were just shooting up blindly.*

I was startled out of my fierce inner monologue by Lilandra's

133

scream. "Jack, watch out!" I looked at Lil and saw her wide eyes staring past me, her hand fumbling inside her cloak for her gun. I had just enough time to turn around and see two massive Palace brutes come bearing down on me. Each one of them was a massive slab of muscle, their tanned flesh covered in a collage of scars and tattoos, marking them out as the warrior caste of the Palace tribe.

What little clothing they did have was tatters of cloth to cover their loins and heavy work boots. But each of them wore a white plastic mask that covered the front of their face, small holes in the front for breathing, and two larger ones for their eyes, which were wide and filled with lust—bloodlust toward me, and another much worse kind of lust for Lilandra. They each carried a massive hunk of rent metal, the end wrapped in cord to form a simple handle. The blades they held were simple and weighty, but incredibly deadly.

I barely managed to duck the swing of the brute who came after me. The other ran past. The lure of supple, pale flesh overwhelmed his battle tactics. Instead of two on one, I only had one brute to deal with, and that meant I went from no chance to a slim chance of survival. I would take that gamble.

My fist flashed upward, scoring a hit in his breadbasket. If I could stun him, even for a few seconds, the fight would be over. Sadly, it seemed he had filled his breadbasket this morning with lead, and my hand jerked back, throbbing. The brute didn't even seem to notice. He was busy yanking his massive blade free of the wall. It snapped free, making the jagged edge even more so, as some metal was left in the wall. He drew the blade above his head and let out a rage-filled roar, and he brought the jagged blade downward, attempting to slice me in twain. I dodged to the left, landing on my side. The blade once more barely missed me. I was getting lucky, but if I didn't do something fast, I knew my luck would run out, and I would eventually be hit. Even a glancing strike would end the fight. I needed to end this, and I saw my chance. My leg shot forward; the heel of my boot cracked into the side of the brute's knee.

A loud, satisfying crunch greeted my ears, followed by another howl from the brute. But this one was of pain, not rage, as his knee bent the wrong way. That leg, despite the massive muscles, was now unable to support his weight, and he crumpled. But he was not dead, and the howl he had issued moments before was answered, coming from somewhere else on this floor. More were coming. I had to end this now.

I reached behind me, grabbing my rifle, and slung it forward. The muscled behemoth threw himself at me from the ground. I fired blindly, but his thick arm slapped the gun away a second later as he landed on me.

Thick, meaty hands locked around my neck. I suddenly found myself unable to breathe. I began to struggle as his head lowered to mine, pressing his white mask to into my face. His hot rancid breath basted my face through the small breathing holes. Spots began to flash before my eyes while I struggled, and my own pulse began to roar in my ears.

I was dying, but death felt so very different than I had assumed it would. I had not expected the heat. My chest and stomach were so hot. Slowly, the dark spots began to fade, and my mind, which had been deprived of oxygen, started to process my thoughts properly. Those massive hands were still clenched around my neck, but their Herculean strength had faded, and those eyes, once filled with the thirst for blood, were now glazed and vacant.

He's dead?

I blinked, trying to understand how. Slowly, I began to heave the massive beast off me, revealing my blood-stained jacket and shirt, and also revealing the ragged hole in the brute's enormous chest. I sat up, blinking, my mind still turning back on after having been choked out. When it did a few seconds later, only one thought filled it. *Lilandra!* My head spun so fast, that for a moment, I thought I might have snapped my own neck, as my vision swam and my neck muscles let out a cry of protest.

I saw her there on the floor, the massive beast of a man crawling onto her, his head lowered like some kind of animal. He smelled her. He groaned and his arousal became evident. Lil stirred slowly, groaning as a gnarled fist came up to gingerly touch the lump on her forehead where his meaty fist had thumped her. I watched her blink, before her own eyes snapped open wide to gaze in horror at the man on top of her.

Her scream was ear piercing, but it pierced my heart more so. I watched her struggle, but his open massive hand was able to grip both her wrists and force her arms above her head. A gurgle, or maybe a laugh, passed through his small mask holes. His free hand slipped down to her ratty jeans. I had to do something. He was going

135

to defile her, right here, right in front of me.

I staggered to my feet and bellowed, "Don't touch her!"

The brute turned his head, as if he was being annoyed by some small fly.

This fly, unfortunately for him, had a bite. I hefted his dead companion's massive jagged blade. It was immensely heavy, but Lilandra's scream and the sight of her lying there gave the strength I needed. Arms shaking with the effort, I brought the blade above my head. And with my own cry of rage, brought it down, wedging the tip of the blade into the center of that muscled back.

The sound of metal shearing into bone was sickening. The brute howled and rolled to his side. His arms flailed, but his legs appeared lifeless. I watched as he struggled in vain to remove the blade wedged in his flesh—but to no avail. I grabbed Lilandra and dragged her to her feet while the beast struggled in his throes. We only had a few moments before the others found our position.

I could see the fear in her eyes. "What are we going to do, Jack?" That normally steady, wonderful voice was now tinged with fear. "Ye can't let them take me, I won't live like that. I can't." Her pitch was rising as the thought of her encounter with the now paralyzed brute brought the terror of what her new life could become if she were caught to the forefront of her thoughts.

I pulled her close and held her. Her body trembled. In another moment, it stopped and I felt her arms around me, holding me. "I won't let them take you. Come on, I have one last idea." I broke our embrace. As she had said before, there would be time for those things later.

I led her to the back of what must have been some kind of storage room. It was filled with shelves, but they and their contents had long ago been removed. But what was still there was the metal hatch on the wall and the small chute behind it. I closed the door behind us and tipped one of the large racks in front of it. It wouldn't hold long once they found us.

"What are we doing here? We're trapped, Jack!" She glanced around, eyes wide like a caged animal.

"No, Lil, listen to me. Behind this hatch is a chute. It leads all the way down to the lower levels. I don't know what it was used for. I tested them using rocks when I was exploring, and they all led to the same room below, which is close to where we need to go. Once there, I know a tunnel which will lead us to an empty building down the street. From there we can make it to your family and their caravan. The Palace won't attack them if there are many of them and armed with the guns we bring. And the Palace won't be down there. They know we are up here and think they have all the ways down covered."

My hand slid into hers, and once more I pulled her close. "I piled rags and cushions from the beds down there, but I haven't yet attached any kind of rope. If we go down there, we'll only be able to slow our fall with our own bodies. There is a chance we could get stuck, or even if we don't, we will be falling too fast and the cushions won't do much."

She leaned up then and kissed me. That surge of energy once again filled me, and this time I could feel her tense up and knew she felt the same thing.

Her lips slowly pulled from mine, and she spoke in hushed sweet tones, "Aye, die we might, but I would rather die alongside ye, than live one moment a slave and without ye."

Our moment was interrupted by three inches of jagged metal puncturing the door. It was yanked free along with chunks of wood. The small sliver of a hole was filled with a bloodshot eye. "Boss, the pretty thing and the runt, they're hiding in here!" The door shuddered. The eye left the hole and was replaced with yet more blade as the old wood yielded to the metal assault.

I led Lilandra to the hatch. The aged metal groaned in protest as I forced it open. The black, yawning pit stood before us, and I felt Lilandra's hand squeeze suddenly. I remembered her fear when she had seen the other, large wire-filled tunnel. This one was much smaller and darker.

I squeezed her hand back and smiled. "Come on, the door won't hold much longer." Her hand slipped from mine. I began to crawl in, feet first. "I'll go first. Perhaps, if I don't make it, you will. If so, you must listen to me. At the bottom, you will leave the room, and make two rights. The hallways are all the same, large gray stone, but at the end of the hall after the second right, once you leave the room, you will see the gray wall is cracked, and behind it is brick and a hole. Go in there and take the farthest tunnel to your left. Follow it straight till you reach a ladder. Climb up. It will lead you into the bottom of another building. Find your way out and onto the street. You should be good from there."

Tears began to run down her soft, pale cheeks while I gave her the directions, and her hand shot to find mine, holding it tightly. "Why are ye doing all of this for me? I only showed up on your doorstep, and now you risk everything for my safety. Why?"

I paused. I knew the answer to the question, and I had known the answer the moment I met her. I gazed up into her fear-filled eyes and whispered softly a tune I had learned from an age long since gone, *"Your eyes they shine so bright, I wanna save that light."*

The fear in those beautiful green eyes melted away, and she murmured back, her voice warm and lyrical, *"I can't escape this now, unless you show me how."*

"How do you know... ?"

"Me Gram used to sing it to me. It is a song passed down from the time before the fall. One only sung in me tribe to those whom we love." She leaned in then, her lips seeking mine for a brief, yet desperate, embrace.

She pulled away quickly. The door was being chipped away and we had no time. "I love ye, Jack, even though we have just met. Should we escape, I shall be yours and you shall be mine."

I started to answer, my heart soaring at her touch and her words, which had mimicked the thoughts within my own heart. But a large chunk of wood flew from the door. A tattooed arm reached inside to try to push away the large metal shelf we had placed in front of it.

"Go, my love, we have little time!"

"I love you too, Lil." I saw her eyes sparkle once, and my fear receded a bit. She loved me and knew I loved her. If I died, at least it was for love. I slid forward and was swallowed by darkness. The last thing I saw was her slim legs sliding into the chute above me as I fell.

*

I sat upon the massive rumbling vehicle. My gaze watched the long line of various other metal machines rumble along a half-covered road leading west toward the mountains. A massive man sat next to me, but unlike the brutes that had almost taken my life, he was clothed in a thick, patchwork cloak, and he had curly, red locks.

He looked down, one good, green eye gazing down at me, the other covered in a simple black eyepatch. He laughed softly and a large warm hand slipped behind my back. "Well, lad, yer one of us now. Me daughter has taken a liking to you, and she tells me that ye saved her life. Welcome to the clan." His laugh was deep and rich and reminded me of Lil's. I sighed and allowed his infectious smile to spread.

A loud roar brought my attention to the side of the moving vehicle. A pair of goggle-covered green eyes looked up at me and winked. With an even louder roar and a belch of fire, Lilandra took off on her smaller, personal, two-wheeled machine. She zipped past us and headed toward the front of the caravan. She was, after all, a scout.

I watched, mesmerized by her whirling hair. It was like watching fire dance, the way it whipped and the sun shone off it. I turned my gaze, for one last time, back to the dwindling city that was Las Vegas, a rotting testament to a time and civilization of excess and grandeur, long since lost.

The sun slowly dipped below the horizon, and as it did, the caravan slowed, people standing atop the old, rusted vehicles as they rumbled along, some even piling out and walking alongside to gaze back upon the cityscape in wonder.

The Excelsior shone brightly in the evening sky. The Jewel of the city once more sparkled after years of lying in darkness. I had left a gift for the Palace tribe, one to ensure they would be distracted from pursuing us. The power line I had connected to the building had only provided power for a few things. All others I had switched off. I had turned them on as we fled. And the Excelsior roared to life. By now every tribe would have descended upon it, attempting to seize and take it for their own. My final gift to the Palace had been the gift of death.

I couldn't help but turn to Lilandra's father, Angus, whose gaze, like everyone else's, was drawn to the tower of light in the distance. His comment about me saving his daughter entered my mind.

I looked out. *That* city, *that* hotel: the Excelsior, which had been my home for years, disappeared behind a curtain of red mountains.

Who had saved who that night?

8

BRIDGE OF GOLD

Rebecca Paisley

PROLOGUE

Las Vegas 1860

The ground split, and the young lady and her little dog disappeared into the chasm. A small group of bearded men, holding their picks, axes and shovels, watched as the open mouth of the land began to close around and over her. She had accompanied them on the long and difficult journey from the foothills of the Tennessee Mountains to the Excelsior Mountains not far from the meadows of Las Vegas, where they searched for gold. And now she had vanished into the thunderous cavern of earth...

The last they saw was the fear in her honey eyes.

Las Vegas 2018

Savio LaFica closed the door of the taxi and gaped at The

Excelsior Hotel, a monstrous mass of ugliness his Uncle Louis had built in 1960. He spied cracks in some upper windows, greasy dirt covering what he assumed used to be white pillars, and a myriad of chips in the tiles upon which he stood. Dusk began to settle over the city, and the Excelsior's lighted sign joined all the others up and down the Strip. But because of the many lights that had burned out, the sign at the top of the fifty-six-year-old edifice spelled E L O R.

So this is what his uncle had done with the fortune he'd made from all things illegal. "Damn." Savio muttered the word, but the sound it made inside him bellowed. He nodded to the bellman who picked up his luggage, then entered through enormous glass doors rimmed in tarnished brass.

The gentleman at the registration desk looked up from his keyboard. The machine seemed more like a video game player than a business computer. "Good afternoon, sir," the man said. "Have you reserved a room here at The Excelsior?" He turned a lamp with a split shade around so the fractured side didn't show.

Savio signed the register. Only a few guests' names appeared on the pages of the book. He decided the people staying here couldn't afford to enjoy the truly elegant hotels Las Vegas offered.

He watched the hotel manager gape at the signature. Surely the man's eyeballs would soon fall out of his head and roll around the empty lobby.

"Mr. La— La—"

"Fica." Savio managed to present a barely-there smile.

"You're— You're Mr. Savio Fica! Louis LaFica's nephew!"

"Yes." Savio stopped smiling.

The man raised his hands to his face, his fingers flittering upon his flushed ears. "I'm Martin Adams, and this is truly an honor! We weren't expecting you, Mr. LaFica, but of course your private suite remains prepared for you at all times in the event you might come to visit."

"Thank you," Savio replied. He saw Mr. Adams glance at the floor several times. Savio looked down too, but he saw only the threadbare emerald carpet. The rug seemed to twinkle a bit. Like gold dust. The shimmer was nice, he thought. Maybe the only pretty thing about the place.

"Our entire staff is at your service," Mr. Adams added.

Well, of course the hotel was at his service, Savio thought. He owned the damn thing. And the sooner it was demolished, the better for all mankind. For that reason alone, Savio had come to Las Vegas. "I appreciate your kindness, Mr. Adams." He shook the man's hand.

Following the bellman into the spacious lobby and toward the elevators, Savio noticed two large gilt-framed paintings above a stone fireplace. Uncle Louis and Louis' mother, Louisa Maria LaFica. Great Aunt Louisa Maria. As he stepped into the elevator, he wondered what the woman had thought about her nefarious son. Poor lady. Then again, perhaps she'd been a vile mother whose wickedness had turned Uncle Louis into the heartless mobster he'd become.

An odd feeling caught him. Ridiculous as he knew it was, he thought he felt his Uncle Louis and Great Aunt Louisa Maria peering at him from within the flaking frames. The sensation was bizarre.

"After you, Mr. LaFica," the bellhop said as they arrived to the penthouse and exited the elevator. The polite young man opened the intricately carved door and immediately stared around the floor. "My name is Ben Adams. The manager here, Martin Adams, is my father. He knew your uncle." Ben kept his gaze on the rug. "I never met Mr. LaFica. May I be of further assistance to you, sir?"

As he'd done in the lobby, Savio glanced at the carpet. There was nothing there but worn emerald tufts with little gold glimmers. "Why are you looking at the floor? Your father did it as well."

Ben lifted his head and stomped his foot on the carpet. "It's nothing, Mr. LaFica. Just making sure the rug is clean for you." He circled his foot around the floor one more time. "We are a bit understaffed at the moment, but I assure you we will do everything we are able to do for you."

A bit understaffed. Savio ran his fingers through his hair. He was well aware there were not many employees working at The Excelsior anymore. He'd let them go one by one, but he'd paid each of them handsomely for their services. A skeleton crew kept the hotel running now. Savio knew they did the best they could, but they too, would have to leave.

When Ben departed, Savio perused the suite, annoyed by the stench of cigarette smoke. The accommodations were as shoddy as the lobby. Visible nail heads polka-dotted the crown molding near the dingy ceiling. The wallpaper was peeling off various sections of the walls. All the seats of the chairs and sofas were indented. Most likely from Uncle Louis' immense weight.

143

Well, this horror of a place would be gone soon, he reminded himself. He would meet with the buyer of the land in a few days to settle the sale and then order the hotel imploded. The city had readily agreed to the destruction. The Excelsior, while once one of the most grand in Las Vegas, was now an eyesore. Savio almost wished his Uncle Louis could be inside while the building sank into the ground.

But the man was already dead. God only knew what Louis had done to bring about his gruesome death. The mob guarded its secrets well. All Savio knew was that about six or so years ago a maid had found Louis' pale and bloodied body in the hotel conference room his uncle had used for clandestine gatherings with his minions. Someone had stabbed a knife into each of his eyes. Perhaps Louis had seen something he shouldn't have seen? Savio shrugged. He had no idea where his uncle was buried. Maybe at the bottom of the ocean with all sorts of sea creatures for company. Wasn't that the Mafia's favorite place to dispose of its victims? Perhaps that was a myth, but Savio liked the way it sounded.

The hotel had certainly fallen into near ruin since Uncle Louis had died. It was just as well, Savio knew. He and his relatives in New York were ashamed to have anything to do with The Excelsior, and with good reason. Uncle Louis had humiliated them all.

Savio settled into a stained satin chair, opened his briefcase and began to read legal agreements. That same peculiar feeling tingled through him again. He dropped his papers into his briefcase and wandered into the huge bedroom. With the exception of a few crooked sconces, one of which didn't work, the only things on the wall were replicas of the portraits of Louis and Louisa Maria LaFica he'd seen downstairs in the lobby. They hung over what appeared to be quite a lumpy bed.

He strode across the room, reached over the bed, and snatched the paintings off the wall. Seized by a violence he wasn't aware he possessed, he slammed each picture over the corner of a dresser. The frames splintered, but the faces of Louis and Louisa Maria remained unscathed. He realized he was acting childishly, but he was too angry to stop. Placing each painting across his knee, he bent them up and down until they broke in half.

"I reckon they're purty much ruined now."

Startled by the sound of a female voice, Savio spun around but saw only empty space and flickers of gold on the carpet. "Who's in

144

here?" he demanded. "Come out!"

"I am out," the soft voice responded. "I'm standing in the bathroom doorway. Did you know there's two bowls in the bathrooms of this here hotel? One's for regular use, but the other one is—"

"I know what a bidet is! Stop hiding! Who are you, where are you, and why are you in my rooms?" Savio turned in a circle again. Golden bits swirled near the bathroom, but he could find no sign of the woman with the silken voice.

Silken voice? Silken voice of a woman he couldn't even see! A woman who had obviously broken into the suite! What the hell was the matter with him? "I'm calling security." He reached for the phone on the scarred bedside table.

"There ain't no security here," the invisible woman said. "Somebody gave them guards some money, and they left. A passel of other folks who worked here got paid and left too. But I don't know who paid them. Was it you?"

Savio couldn't speak.

"There was a time I'd try to learn everything that went on here, but I figure I've done learned enough," the woman continued. "I already know about airplanes and fast cars. And machines that throw out drinks and nibbles. One of them machines makes ice. When I first got here I played with ice every day."

"Ice," Savio repeated.

"Yeah, ice. It really dilled my pickle to do that. I also know a man walked on the moon, but I still ain't figured out why he didn't fall off into all that heaven space. I know what television is too. When I first saw a television I thought everything I watched was really inside the box. But now I know that ain't true. Them pictures come through on wires, or something like that. Not many folks come here anymore," she added and took a breath. "So mostly I just try and hide from Louis, that devil. He still has them knifes in his eyes, and his face is always covered with blood. He's going to haunt me to no dang end."

As he listened to the woman's non-stop chatter, Savio wondered what she was talking about. His Uncle Louis? Blood? Louis was dead! The woman was daft. Was her talking coming from a speaker? Considering his uncle's depraved line of work, it made sense that listening devices, old as they might be, were scattered throughout the hotel.

But how did the woman know what he was doing? She'd commented on his destroying the paintings. Maybe there were cameras installed here and there too. Yes, it sounded just like something a member of the mob would have done.

"You look like him," the woman went on. "Course, you don't weigh no three hundred pounds like he does. But your black hair curls around your forehead like his do, and your brown eyes and skin are dark like his. But you're a right handsome fellow. Louis? Well, Louis looks like he fell out of the ugly tree and hit every branch on the way down."

Savio didn't miss the fact that she spoke in the present tense. As if Louis were still alive. He inhaled deeply and clenched his hands into fists. "Wherever you are, come to my room so I can see you."

"Say please."

"Please!"

"You ain't got to yell at me when I ain't done a thing to you. Here I come."

Savio turned to watch the room door, but no one opened it.

"Here," the woman said. "Here I am, near the bathroom door like I done told you."

His mouth fell open. His heart punched his chest.

Clad in a gossamer gown, a slight and glorious figure stepped out from within a cloud of gold gleam.

Chapter Two

"What— Who—" Savio couldn't find any more words.

"What am I?" the woman asked. "Who am I?" She approached him, grinning when he took a few steps backwards. But he didn't seem afraid, she decided. Confused, but not truly scared.

Was this the brave man she'd hoped for? She dared not believe such a wonderful thing. "Savio," she whispered, trying with all her might to ignore her hungry curiosity. If he wasn't frightened now, she sure didn't want him to be. "Savio LaFica."

His name sounded like a melody on her lips, but Savio fought the temptation to fall under the mysterious spell she'd somehow tangled around him. He wanted to grab the tangle and throw it across the room.

But he couldn't do it.

"Are you going to back and forth with me, Savio?"

"Back and forth?" He saw her lay her hand upon her cheek. Her movement was the most graceful thing he'd ever imagined could exist.

."Your mouth keeps opening like a fish. Like you might be fixing to tell me something. Maybe something real important." She waited for him to tell her he was her savior.

Savio closed his mouth so quickly he bit his tongue. "Dammit!" Swiping at his lips, he backed away again and fell into the chair behind him. He was tired, he reasoned. Hallucinating. Yes. That happened when people were exhausted. He'd worked long and hard at his office in New York that morning. Then he'd rushed to the airport, where his private plane waited to fly him to Vegas.

"You ain't seeing fake things, Savio." She neared his chair and blew a few gold bubbles away from her face. "Everybody thinks that. I'm real is what I am. Well, not real, really. But I ain't dead, and I ain't no ghost neither. I'm alive as I can possibly be after spending a hundred years in that deep ditch that swallowed me up. Strange thing was that me and my friends the gold diggers came here from the foothills of the Excelsior Mountains, and now this here hotel is named The Excelsior. Real spooky that Louis built this hotel right on the very spot I fell into the ditch and got closed into the earth. And I didn't never get old. Ain't that something?"

"A hundred years?" Wasn't that part of a fairy tale he'd read as a child? Savio stared at the woman so hard, his eyes stung. She seemed as delicate as a baby's sigh. Her long gold hair fell over her shoulders like a glistening veil, and her skin was translucent. Fair, yes, but surely she'd been kissed by a sunbeam.

And her eyes... Not brown. Tawny. Like honey.

Honey eyes. He could not stop himself from gazing into them. She smiled at him.

He knew he'd never seen a smile like hers. Her mouth was as silky as her voice.

"Name's Honeybee."

"Honey." Savio murmured the name while his mind tried to understand what else to do. His body knew exactly what he wanted to do. Dammit! He'd only just met this exquisite woman, and he already wanted her. Maybe he was daft as she was.

"Honeybee," she told him again and lifted her arm to hold out her little hand.

He saw gold beads in her palm. But they vanished almost as soon as he looked at them. Slowly, he reached out and touched her fingers, ready to pull back his arm if need be. Like if she caught him on fire, or something like that.

But her skin was as silky as her mouth and voice. His fingers curled around hers before he realized what he was doing. He yanked his hand away. "Look, lady," he snapped. "I don't know who the hell you—"

"Name's not Lady. It's Honeybee. Done told you that two times already." She leaned down to him. "I've seen many a man since Louis built this place some fifty or so years ago. Italian men. But dang. Not an Italian like you. You don't hurt my eyes nary a bit. And you're tall. So tall I reckon if you fell down you'd be halfway home."

When he caught himself wondering if she liked tall men or not, he stood and glared down at her. "I have no inkling what you're talking about!"

"I'm fixing to tell you if you stop hollering at me." She cocked her head toward her shoulder. "You deserve to know, see, because you ain't afraid of me like some folks are when they see me." She glided to the bed and sat on it. "Most guest folks scream and run. Or faint. Or can't move at all. I never mean to scare nobody, but I can't help the way I am. And that dang Louis? Well, he won't let me out of this dang hotel. Every time I try to escape, he's there blocking me and pulling me away. And he's all the time trying to grab me. And kiss me with them big wet lips he's got."

She reached for a pillow and hugged it. "You know how he got that name, Louis 'The Lip' LaFica?" She waited for Savio to answer, but he remained in astonished silence. "Most folks think that name comes from those blubber lips of his. But that ain't it. His mama used to be here too, you know, but I ain't seen her in many a year. I'm purty sure she died for real, but I'm wrong sometimes. Not a lot, but sometimes.

"Anyhow," she continued, "even though Louis was a grown man, his mama would say, 'Don't give me any lip, Louis!' She said that when he was being sarcastic or when he talked back to her. Lots of his crooked varmint friends heard her. And they gave him that name, see. Louis 'The Lip' LaFica. He hates that name so I call him that as many times as I can. It makes him madder than a mule chewing on wasps."

"Wait. Just wait." Savio rubbed his forehead while still staring at her. "Are you trying to tell me my uncle... He's here? Alive? And if you aren't dead or alive or a ghost, then what the hell are you?"

She lifted one eyebrow.

It looked like an upside down smile to Savio. He wanted to touch more than her fingers. Dear God, what was this power she held over him? He'd only just met her!

Now he felt furious with his own self.

"I'm between the layers of alive, dead, and ghostly," Honeybee informed him. "But Louis? He's a ghost for sure and certain. He got himself killed by one of them no-good friends of his. That man sure weren't no friend, huh? Louis had knifes sticking out—"

"I know how he died!"

His shouting irritated her again. "Well, if you know so dang much, then why'd you ask—"

"Okay." Savio pulled in a very deep breath, struggling to make himself believe all of this was truly happening to him. "All right. Why don't we start at the beginning? What ditch? A hundred years? How did you get here? Who are you really? Where are you from?"

She stretched out on the bed and looked at the crumbling ceiling. "I'm stuck here, Savio. Not only does Louis stop me from leaving, but I don't think I could leave even if he weren't looking. I was standing on this very spot of land a hundred years ago. Me and my little dog."

He heard her trembling breath. "Are you crying?"

"My dog."

He saw her tears and wanted to kiss them away. How was it possible for him to go from impatience to desire so fast? He gave up trying to battle his feelings. He felt them, and that was that. "Where is your dog?"

"He fell into the ground with me. Blue. His name was Blue because his eyes was the color of the sky. The rest of him was tan. When Louis broke ground to build this hotel, me and Blue saw the hole. We scrambled out of it but didn't know where we was. Didn't seem like nobody could see us, and we was so afraid. Everything was different. I saw things I never saw before. So me and Blue? We stayed right here and watched this place get built around us. When it was done getting built, Louis strutted around and thought the sun came up just to hear him crow."

"And he captured you?" Savio tried so hard to understand.

"He didn't really capture us. We just couldn't leave. Maybe it was evil magic that kept us here." She sat up and looked at Savio. "At first Louis was the only one who thought he saw us, but then other people saw us too. The Excelsior got known as a ghost hotel. Some guests left afraid for their lives, but others hung around hoping they could see me and Blue again. I tried to stay vanished, but these dang sparkles won't get off me and, well, it's hard for me to be all the way disappeared, see."

No, Savio didn't see. But he was beginning to believe her. Wild as her story was, what other conclusion could he make? He sat down beside her. "You were down in the lobby when I arrived, weren't you? The manager and his son saw your sparkles and tried to keep me from noticing them."

Honeybee liked the way his body warmed her own. Feelings she'd never experienced warmed her even more. "Yeah. The workers know I'm here. I'm special friends with Mr. Adams and his son, Ben. They're good folks. I'll be sorry to see them leave. I reckon one day soon I'll be all alone here. Except for Louis. He's going to chase me until I truly die."

Savio felt instantly guilty and worried. What would happen to Honeybee when the employees were gone and the hotel was destroyed? Would Louis really follow her wherever she went? The questions bothered him deeply. But maybe he could think of a way to get her out of the hotel before the planned implosion. He'd certainly try.

He didn't want anything to happen to this golden imp. "How did you get your name. Honeybee? I've never known anyone with that name."

"My daddy gave it to me on account of my gold hair. Daddy thought I looked like a honeybee. Honeybee Darcy's my whole name. We lived in the mountains of Tennessee. Daddy and Mama died, though. When they was gone, I left Tennessee with some neighbor men who was going west to look for gold. Lots of gold."

Tennessee, Savio thought. That explained the way she spoke and the phrases she used to describe things. "How did you stay alive in the ground for a hundred years?"

"Magic," she repeated to him. "Couldn't be nothing else."

Savio didn't believe in magic. Before tonight, anyway. Now he wondered if it might be true. He sorted through everything Honeybee had told him. It no longer mattered to him that he didn't understand.

But she mattered. In the space of a bit over an hour, she'd come to matter to him. "All right. Now, why are you surrounded by the shimmer?"

She caught some golden sprinkles in her hand. "Only thing I can think of is that there was gold in the ground that ate me and Blue. Them gold twinkles got on me and came up with me and Blue when we saw the hole that was getting dug."

Savio nodded as if her story made perfect sense to him. "What about Blue? Where is he?"

Honeybee had tears in her eyes again. "Blue was a fast runner. He stayed here with me until the hotel was ready for guests. But Louis hated dogs and forced Blue out the doors. Blue looked at me through the glass down in the lobby. He stayed in front of them doors for a long time. Days. I finally told him to go on. About killed me to do it, but I couldn't let him be there forever, you know? Ain't seen him since. But I heard about this bridge? Well, it's made out of a rainbow. Pets cross over that bridge, and then their people go and—"

"Honeybee, the Rainbow Bridge is only a story."

"Why? There's magic everywhere. Ain't I proof of that?"

Savio had to admit to himself that she had a point.

151

"'Course, everything around me is gold," Honeybee mused aloud. "So maybe that bridge ain't made of no rainbow. Maybe it's gold."

A golden bridge. Savio knew exactly where one was.

She peered up at him and touched his chest.

For some reason he didn't bother to fathom, he reached out and held her within the circle of his arms.

And it dawned on him how right it was to have her there.

Chapter Three

The next morning Honeybee was gone. She'd fallen asleep beside Savio during the night. He dressed quickly, but before he left his room for the lobby he saw the portraits hanging above the bed again. He knew full well Honeybee would not have placed them on the wall again.

Well, Honeybee believed in magic. He might as well too. "Uncle Louis." He stared at the painting and felt not at all ridiculous about speaking to a portrait. "For years you have committed unspeakable crimes. And you've made Honeybee miserable. Well, not anymore, uncle. You're a ghost whose soul remains here in your atrocity of a hotel. But I'm alive. And I'm going to send you straight to hell." He pulled the painting off the wall and smashed it again before walking to the door, opening it, and slamming it shut.

"Mr. Adams," he said when he reached the desk. "Have you seen the gold dust on the floor today?"

"What? Uh, what gold dust, Mr. LaFica? I'm sure I don't know what—"

"Yes, you do." Savio leaned against the marred desk and smiled a real smile. "I met her last night. The golden girl. Honeybee Darcy. Have you seen her or her sparkles?"

Mr. Adams returned Savio's smile with a big one of his own. "So you know."

"Everything."

The manager nodded. "Beautiful girl. Sweet. The entire Excelsior staff loves her. Your uncle... We no longer call him Louis 'The Lip' LaFica. Very simply, we call him SOB Ghost. But it's been awhile since he's bothered her. We believe he's gone, thank the good Lord."

"He's not gone. He glared at me from that damn painting on the wall. Yesterday."

"What? Yesterday?" Mr. Adams blanched and wrung his hands. "Now that you've mentioned it, Honeybee is late with her morning greeting visit, Mr. LaFica! She always comes to keep me company, but I haven't seen her all morning! Oh, God! He must be back, just like you said! He's after her!"

Savio straightened. He's after her. The manager's words sliced through him. Stiff with worry, he searched the lobby for signs of

Honeybee. He didn't see a single gold twinkle.

"The... The conference room where he was killed!" Mr. Adams covered his face with his hands. "It's a terrible room! I can almost see blood everywhere!"

"Where's the room?" Savio shouted.

"You're going to go there?"

"Where Is The Room?" Savio yelled again.

"It's the very bottom of the hotel! Press zero in the elevator! He—"

Savio ran to the elevator before the manager finished speaking. He jabbed at the zero button. When the door opened on the bottom floor, he quickly found the conference room and stormed inside.

Sure enough, Louis had Honeybee pushed against the wall, his fat hands fondling her breasts. Knives pierced his eyes. Blood dripped down his face. "Louis, you son of a bitch!"

When the pale ghost turned around, his shoulder knocked a painting of his mother off the wall. He kicked the portrait away and tightened his arms around Honeybee.

"Savio! He ain't never gone this far! Help—"

"Shut your stupid mouth, you dirty whore," Louis growled. "You've had me chasing you for years. This time you aren't going to escape me! And you can blame your lover boy. No one will have you but me!"

What Savio saw heightened his fury and hatred. Louis was not only attempting to kiss Honeybee. . .

He was trying to rape her.

Savio reached Louis and Honeybee in three long strides. He tried to pull his uncle away from Honeybee, to no avail.

Louis laughed a horrible guttural sound. "She's mine, Savio. You can never take her from me!"

Savio's powerful rage gave him strength he'd never felt before. Again, he reached for Louis. This time he managed to haul the ghost away from Honeybee. "Honeybee, run and get Mr. Adams and Ben to help you get to the airport!" With all his power he was able to hold his enraged uncle. "Go to my plane, and take Mr. Adams and Ben with you! Go to San Francisco! Go to the bridge, Honeybee! Go to the Golden Bridge!"

She hesitated.

"Go!" Savio fought his squirming uncle. "Go, Honeybee! Run!"

Louis laughed again. "She can't leave!" His blood smeared down Savio's shirt, and the knives in his eyes shook as he chortled. "She can never leave, Savio! Never!"

At that moment Savio realized he knew of something mightier than his uncle's inhuman strength. "I love you, Honeybee! I love you! I promise to meet you at the bridge! Now, go!"

Horror slammed into her as she watched Louis grab one of the knives out of his eye socket and plunge it into Savio's chest. "Savio!" Tears almost blinded her. "I can't—"

"Yes." Savio fought the gruesome pain. "Please," he gritted between his teeth. "Please, Honeybee."

She heard the desperation in his quiet plea and knew she had to grant what might be his last wish. Her heart shattered into bits as she turned and fled.

Savio watched her until she disappeared. "I love her," he whispered to his uncle. "Kill that, you damn demon."

Louis' cheerfulness faded instantly. He yanked the other knife from his eye, poised to stab his nephew again.

"Louis, stop this immediately!"

It was a woman's voice Savio heard. Before he surrendered to his pain he could have sworn he saw the painting on the floor move.

But all he could think of was that he was going to break his promise to Honeybee.

He closed his eyes and waited for death.

*

Honeybee wept into Mr. Adams' shoulder during the entire flight to San Francisco. Sorrow such as she'd never known choked her and left her breathless. She could not even think upon the facts that she'd escaped The Excelsior and was flying in Savio's plane.

He was dead. He'd saved her as he was dying. He wouldn't be meeting her at the bridge of gold. And she'd not had the chance to tell him she loved him too. Her sobs became louder.

"Oh, Honeybee." Ben patted her arm. "Oh, Honeybee."

When the plane landed at the San Francisco airport, Mr. Adams and Ben hurried Honeybee through the terminal and outside to the taxi curb. The three of them got into a cab.

"The Golden Gate Bridge!" Mr. Adams yelled at the taxi driver.

Honeybee didn't remember the drive. She alighted from the car when it stopped in front of the biggest bridge she'd ever seen. Sunshine sparkled all over the structure. It wasn't made of a rainbow. Savio was right. No Rainbow Bridge existed. She hung her head and noticed her gold dust was gone. She was truly in the real world now.

But it meant nothing without Savio to share it with her.

"He'll be here, Honeybee," Mr. Adams tried to reassure her.

Ben nodded. "Yes, he will. He's probably on his way right now."

But hope eluded all three of them before Honeybee remembered to cross the bridge. Crossing was part of the story!

The majestic bridge swayed in front of her. Gold, just like she'd wondered it might be. "I have to cross it. The story—"

"It's very long, Honeybee," Ben said.

"Over a mile," Mr. Adams added. "You can't walk that far, Honeybee. You're exhausted. And look at all the traffic." He put his arm around her waist.

She walked out of his embrace. And she kept walking, her gaze never leaving the tremendous bridge. Her love for Savio surged through her as she found the path along the side of the bridge. She began to walk faster. And faster, until she was running. Gulping air, she continued her journey.

She didn't care if crossing the bridge took forever, she decided as she ran.

But forever didn't come. She did, indeed, reach the end of the bridge. Panting, she searched for anything that moved in front of her. Anything but cars. Something she might recognize.

But she saw no familiar thing and knew then that Savio was truly gone. If he'd had any breath left in his body, he would have somehow found a way to meet her.

He'd promised her. She fell to her knees and cried anew.

A sound broke through her loud weeping. What sound? She lifted her head but still saw nothing she recognized on the shore.

But the sound became louder.

A bark.

Not daring to breathe for fear the sound would fade, Honeybee rose to her feet and squinted at the land.

There came a man toward her. He held a wiggling thing is his arms. She heard the bark again.

Blue! It was Blue!

Savio began to run, clutching the barking dog to his chest.

"Oh, dear Lord in heaven!" Honeybee yelled."Savio!" She, too, began to run.

And then they reached each other. "Savio, I—"

"Aunt Louisa Maria," Savio told her. "She came to life in the painting!" He handed the happy, excited dog to her.

"What? What do you mean?" She didn't know who to hug first. Man or dog.

"She stopped Louis from stabbing me with his second knife!" Savio grinned. "She came to life, Honeybee. My aunt. She jerked Louis into the frame with her and told him not to give her any lip. Once he had disappeared into the painting with her, she spoke to me. She said she'd waited for many years for Louis to find true love, but that he preferred strumpets who only desired his money."

"But all the blood. Your wounds."

"Honeybee, they vanished after Aunt Louisa Maria wished you and me well and said goodbye!" He looked into her honeyed eyes. "We're going to rebuild the hotel. It will be the grandest on the Strip. We'll bring back all the employees who lost their jobs. And we'll rename the hotel too."

She saw the twinkle in his dark eyes. "What will we name it?"

He smoothed his finger across one of her tawny eyebrows. "The Honeybee, of course!" He pulled her closer to him. "You're real. As real as I am." He felt warm tears fill his eyes and splash down his face. "I fell in love with you the moment you stepped out of your golden sparkles the evening we met."

"I love you too, Savio. With all my very real heart."

Savio bent toward her face and gently touched his lips to hers.

Honeybee smiled, her mouth still clinging to his. "My first kiss," she whispered to him while her precious dog licked her neck. "But ... But how did you get here so quickly, Savio? We left Las Vegas before you were able to, and the airplane ride felt very long."

He pressed another kiss into the golden silk of her hair. "There's good magic too, Honeybee. You said so yourself. A wonderful and amazing magic."

"Love," she answered. "Magic."

And with Blue nestled between them, Savio and Honeybee embraced.

Upon the Bridge of Gold.

13Thirty Books

Exciting Thrillers, Heart-Warming Romance,
Mind-Bending Horror, Sci-Fantasy
and
Educational Non-Fiction

The Third Hour

The Third Hour is an original spin on the religious-thriller genre, incorporating elements of science fiction along with the religious angle. Its strength lies in this originality, combined with an interesting take on real historical figures, who are made a part of the experiment at the heart of the novel, and the fast pace that builds.

Ripper – A Love Story

"Queen Victoria would not be amused--but you will be by this beguiling combination of romance and murder. Is the Crown Prince of England really Jack the Ripper? His wife would certainly like to know… and so will you."
Diana Gabaldon, New York Times Best Selling Author

Heather Graham's Haunted Treasures

Presented together for the first time, New York Times Bestselling Author, Heather Graham brings back three tales of paranormal love and adventure.

Heather Graham's Christmas Treasures

New York Times Bestselling Author, Heather Graham brings back three out-of-print Christmas classics that are sure to inspire, amaze, and warm your heart.

Zodiac Lovers Series

Zodiac Lovers is a series of romantic, gay, paranormal novelettes. In each story, one of the lovers has all the traits of his respective zodiacal sign.

Never Fear

Shh… Something's Coming

Never Fear – Phobias

Everyone Fears Something

Never Fear – Christmas Terrors

He sees you when you're sleeping …

More Than Magick

Why me? Recent college grad Scott Madison, has been recruited (for reasons that he will eventually understand) by the wizard Arion and secretly groomed by his ostensible friend and mentor, Jake Kesten. But his training hasn't readied him to face Vraasz, a being who has become powerful enough to destroy the universe and whose first objective is the obliteration of Arion's home world. Scott doesn't understand why he was the chosen one or why he is traveling the universe with a ragtag group of individuals also chosen by Arion. With time running out, Scott discovers that he has a power that can defeat Vraasz. If only he can figure out how to use it.

Stop Saying Yes – Negotiate!

Stop Saying Yes - Negotiate! is the perfect "on the go" guide for all negotiations. This easy-to-read, practical guide will enable you to quickly identify the other side's tactics and strategies allowing you to defend yourself ensuring a better negotiation for your side and theirs.

13Thirtybooks.com
facebook.com/13thirty

Made in the USA
Middletown, DE
15 June 2016